Fierce as the Wind

ALSO BY TARA WILSON REDD

The Museum of Us

Fierce as the Wind

TARA WILSON REDD

This is a work of fiction. Names, characters, places, and incidents either are the product of the author's imagination or are used fictitiously. Any resemblance to actual persons, living or dead, events, or locales is entirely coincidental.

 Published in the United States by Wendy Lamb Books, an imprint of Random House Children's Books, a division of Penguin Random House LLC, New York.

Wendy Lamb Books and the colophon are trademarks of Penguin Random House LLC.

Visit us on the Web! GetUnderlined.com

Educators and librarians, for a variety of teaching tools, visit us at RHTeachersLibrarians.com

Library of Congress Cataloging-in-Publication Data is available upon request.
ISBN 978-1-5247-6691-7 (trade) — ISBN 978-1-5247-6692-4 (lib. bdg.) —
ISBN 978-1-5247-6693-1 (ebook)

The text of this book is set in 11.75-point Adobe Garamond Pro.
Interior design by Andrea Lau

Printed in the United States of America
10 9 8 7 6 5 4 3 2 1
First Edition

For my sister, Halle

For Alexander, always

I know it's bad for me to keep remembering, and yet
You're not so easy to forget!

"You're Not So Easy to Forget,"
by Ben Oakland and Herb Magidson
from *Song of the Thin Man*

—

Now I understand
What you tried to say to me

"Vincent," by Don McLean

IMPOSSIBLE

chapter one

I am racing. The wind sings in my ears and burns my tearstained cheeks as I fly down the hill on my bike. The sky is starless, moonless, empty. My headlight cuts a yellow circle out of the night ahead of me, just enough to find my way.

There's a part of my brain that talks when I bike this hard, while the rest of my mind is perfectly still. Tonight, it wants me to notice the palm trees and the brush as my headlight passes over them. Even though I am blinded by rage, I see Van Gogh's rolling cypress trees in the scraggly branches. The voice remembers how Van Gogh's ink sketches of those trees look like towering bonfires. The voice sees so much beauty in the world.

But as I skid to a stop, it goes silent.

I'm here.

I steer straight into the bushes, cutting up my legs.

I bunny hop my bike over roots until I'm hidden in the trees. The ground gets sandier, less stable, with fallen branches and trash all over. Even though I'm fighting as hard as I can, my front wheel finally gets caught in a rut too deep to push through, and the bike starts to fall sideways. I jump off before I go down with it.

I find a sturdy-looking tree trunk and chain up my bike. I take off my helmet, hang it on the handlebars. I unstrap my pillowcase full of heartache from my rack. The bungee cord snaps back into my arm, and I let out a yelp. I sling the pillowcase over my shoulder.

On foot, I break through the trees out onto the beach. My pillowcase is stabbing me in the back as I make my way toward the oil drum down on the sand. I shift my cursed load. My legs are on fire from cranking over here, and I can't catch my breath.

I stop when I get to the oil drum, the only thing on this stretch of beach. I drop my pillowcase in the sand. I wipe the sweat from my eyes and I check my phone. Still no answer. My last seven text messages form a column on my side of the conversation. I clench my teeth and slide my phone away so I can turn the pillowcase upside down into the oil drum.

Most of what he gave me over two years was paper: books, notebooks, an occasional postcard. Everything else was digital. We spent two years together in WhatsApp and Snapchat. We rode wolves across the wild pixelated fields of *Eldritch Codex,* controllers in hand, me and my partner in crime. We were miles apart but always together. But it was the books I treasured. The books were really him. I dump in his copy of Van Gogh's letters, illuminated by his commentary in the margins, his chicken-scratch thoughts in French and English, in Latin and Greek, connections only he could have made. Into the drum go the novels, the sketchbooks and Moleskines he inscribed to me, every bookmark and every poem and every bit of mail from abroad. I dump in every Post-it note I saved because his handwriting was precious to me.

Even paper drenched with tears burns when you squirt a full container of lighter fluid over it. I scream as I shake every drop from the bottle. I reach into my pocket and . . .

And . . .

I don't have a lighter.

~

It's the middle of the night, but I jump back on my bike and ride the full twenty miles back to the Trailer Park. The wind is against me now and it takes forever.

My house isn't actually a trailer, but it squeaks like one. I try to silently swing open the front screen door. It screams like it always does.

Achilles gallops out from his post in my room, thundering down the hall past my dad's bedroom. I raise a finger to my lips, holding my hand out flat and willing the word "Stay" into his defective Shiba Inu consciousness. Achilles has three-fourths the number of legs of a standard-issue dog, and one-fourth the brain. I pray he is in a listening mood.

He sits, cocks his head at me, and watches as I slide open the kitchen junk drawer so smoothly that nothing inside it moves. I withdraw a book of matches that reads "Uncle Tua's Pizzeria" without touching anything else in the drawer. I can see the long grill lighter buried in the bottom, but there's no way I can reach it without disturbing approximately a million keys that open nothing. *Jeez, Dad,* I think. How do old people accumulate so many dead batteries and keys?

Achilles is looking at me like he thinks I've been hiding his long-lost pink tennis ball in that drawer all along, holding out on him. I keep my hand up, but he's losing patience. He starts to whine, hopping around, bouncing back and forth on his one front leg.

"Down, Achilles!" I whisper-shout. In reply, he barks louder than you would think possible for such a small dog.

I stand absolutely still, one foot hovering aloft as I wait.

"Aki-chan!" growls my dad from his room in the back. Achilles goes running off to appease his real master. As Dad is grumbling at the dog, I back my way silently to the door.

And then I am gone, racing away.

Without a giant pillowcase, it only takes me an hour or so to ride back, even in the dark. The wind is with me again, pushing me forward.

As I chain my bike up, I wonder how many miles I've gone tonight. I've always wanted one of those bike computers that tells you your distance, your pace, but I'll never be able to afford one. I know these roads so well, though, I can guess: over a hundred, racing from truth to truth, discovery to discovery. I'm so full of adrenaline I can't even feel the miles.

That's almost far enough to loop the whole island and end up right back where I started: a snake eating its own tail. *Ouroboros,* my brain helpfully suggests. He wrote a paper on that symbol and its use in different cultures for his history term paper last semester. I proofread it.

I stop. I look at my phone. Still no reply.

He's not going to answer me. Two years, and I don't even get an explanation?

I head down to the beach, fighting back the tears.

My oil drum is untouched. I look down. I see how one of his books spreads open and crumples, the way the rust looks on the inside of the oil drum, tracing the ribs of it, eating away holes. That book sitting in a rusty oil drum says everything about this night. That's the only way I could ever explain what this feels like: by putting it into colors and lines. And I want so badly to show someone what I see, because what I see is what I feel.

Except, the someone I want to show everything to is the whole reason I'm out here.

I turn away from the oil drum, my eyes on the ground. My sneakers.

He got them for me at the Van Gogh Museum, printed with the moody blues and yellows of *Wheatfield with Crows.*

I sit down in the sand and yank them off. I leap up and dangle them over the oil drum. They spin from their laces.

I will my hand to let go, but my hand won't do it.

"Let go," I say out loud. It takes all of my strength to open my fist and let them drop. As they land on the pile of books and papers, it should sound like a volcano. But it sounds like what it is: a pair of cheap sneakers being thrown away.

I pull out the matches. My hands are shaking as I light one, carefully guarding its tiny flame from the wind. I drop it into the oil drum and watch everything burn.

chapter two

Even in permadamp Hawai'i, my California roots won't let me walk away from the fire until I've drowned it dead with seawater, which I have to carry up to the oil drum in one of the plentiful discarded beer cans on the beach. By that time, I'm exhausted. Without shoes, it's a long way back to my bike, picking my way through the trees. I'm almost calm as I walk toward the headlight. I stow my lock and make my way patiently to the road with my bike over my shoulder, walking carefully on the uneven ground.

Back on the gravel path, I can tell something is wrong with my bike as soon as I set it down. I pop off the headlight to look at the wheels.

Both flat. Completely flat.

I lock my bike up and hide it in the trees as best I can. I have a spare tube, but not for both tires. I'm stuck.

I take out my phone.

My fingers automatically pull up his contact, like muscle memory. If I told him I was alone in the middle of the night on a deserted practically-made-for-murder road, would he come and get me? Is he even getting these messages?

I want so desperately to text him: message eight on my side of the column. But I know in my heart that even though on Wednesday he told me he loved me, and on Thursday he kissed me goodbye, today is the first Friday of forever and he is a ghost.

As of today, he's gone back to the person he always cared for.

He might have even known he was leaving me yesterday, I realize. Maybe even the day before. Maybe he's known for weeks and he kept on lying so I would keep sleeping with him. I'll probably never know how far back the lies go. Even my heart is cringing. How could I be so stupid? How could I not see?

I scroll away from his number. I text X to come get me. He'll be up before dawn. He has to get up at four a.m. our time so his mentor at Google in California can talk with him once a week at seven a.m. before work.

X won't see the message for three hours. He won't be free for four. I hit send anyway.

The text sits there, claiming it is outgoing, refusing to move.

I look at the bars. No reception.

Typical.

I want to scream.

Now I'm starting to feel it, the hangover from wrath. But I need a ride, and that means getting to a signal. My legs are Jell-O after biking all night. Even so, I start walking toward the nearest town.

~

An hour of walking feels like days. The streetlights seem to be miles apart. Through some small miracle, I have not cut my feet on anything. At last, I'm on the edge of town, on the beach. All the beaches in Hawai'i are public, even the ones in front of the Disney resort. So even though there's one of those mega high-rise condo things ruining the landscape, I'm not trespassing. I'm obviously underage, though, so the chances of getting picked up for breaking curfew are high. I need to hide.

Right in front of me, nearly glowing like a resource in a video game that the designers want you to find, there's a bench on a concrete slab in the sand. Hanging over it, there's some kind of plastic sheet. When I get close, I see that it's a banner ad with metal-rimmed holes where it should have been tied to something. Maybe a homeless person used it as part of a tent. Given the lack of homeless people on this beach, it seems likely that they all got rounded up last night. Maybe the cops won't come back for another sweep.

I sit down and curl my knees to my chest to get my feet off the sand. It's not that cold out—even February isn't cold here—but I'm cold, maybe because my clothes are still soaked with sweat from riding. I should be exhausted, but I can't sleep.

I pull out my phone. Blessed bars, full reception. I resend the text to X. Then I wait, thinking maybe that coward's last words are downloading from space, and there's some reasonable explanation I simply haven't thought of.

Nothing.

There won't ever be a reply. Somehow, after I burned it all, I just know.

I know I'm making it worse. I can't help it.

I pull up her Instagram account.

There it is: all the evidence that was too cruel for me to even imagine.

Pictures of her in her marching band uniform with its ridiculous hat, posing with her flute in a gaggle of girls. I know that field. I made out with him under the bleachers where she is standing. Pictures of her at swim practice. Pictures of her on her bike. Pictures of her in running shorts. Pictures of her with comically large medals on one of those stage things with three heights, or maybe she is tiny, waving like a beauty queen. #swimbikerun #fitfam #girlswhotri #imtraining. Three hundred likes. Twenty-seven comments telling her how cute she is in her sports bra.

Pictures of Hawai'i. Her Hawai'i is the Hawai'i of postcards. Pictures of her year abroad in Japan last year. Pictures of her cat. Pictures of hiking, of Europe, of her college acceptance packet full of confetti. Pictures of her and her friends.

He's there and he's not. He's there, a pair of Sperry Top-Siders on the edge of the pool at her swim meet. He's there, a pair of crossed arms sitting across from her marching band hat at Starbucks. He's there, holding the camera. He's always just out of frame.

I don't like to be in pictures. Neither does he. I only have one picture of us together: it's his feet in his ratty blue high tops and my feet in my Van Gogh sneakers. I took a picture of our feet when we were standing so close he had to wrap his arms around me so I didn't fall backward, my phone wedged between us. I look at that picture now and I remember exactly how he smelled, how the sun felt on my hair, how I could feel his heart beating. I never take photos because they never feel like the moment they were taken. I can't make a picture talk the way I can make paint talk. But that one, it speaks.

I want to delete it, but I've destroyed so much tonight. My fingers won't do it. Besides, even though I hate myself for it, I want that picture. It's the only one I have.

I would give anything for a photo of him now. I could draw him, but it wouldn't be real in the same way. Art may be truth, but photographs are evidence. I want something to hold in my hands and soak with my tears. I wish I had a real photo, just one, of him and me. I wish I could prove I was there, that I was his total sucker of a side chick, and not some delusional psycho who he never even knew and definitely never dated.

But I don't have one, so instead I scour her Instagram. Girls like her take so many pictures, and people take so many pictures of them. I have plenty to look at. A picture jumps out from the rest, like a car swerving out of its lane right at me. It hurts how I imagine getting hit on my bike would hurt: an unexpected jolt, then flying, then impact, all at the slow speed of disbelief.

One of her posts is a Boomerang of two pairs of feet, a giant flat-screen television in the background. *The Thin Man* is playing on the screen, and William Powell is perpetually raising his glass to his lips and setting it down again. She must have been sitting on his lap to take the picture. The feet dance back and forth as the video loops. The post is captioned "Thin Man binge with The Boy. #nickandnora #partnersincrime." It was posted two days before my birthday last year. I scroll through my text messages. That night, I asked what he was up to. He texted back, "geology bleh" and a gif of a bored sloth wearing glasses.

I want to cry, but I'm all cried out. The wind over the waves still sounds like it's crying, and it's like the world has taken the baton so I don't have to keep it up. I close her social media. I can't take any more tonight. I want music, but my phone is almost dead. I text X my GPS location just in case and put my phone in my backpack, putting it under my head. I wrap the big banner over my bench to shelter me from the wind and hopefully the cops if they come by. I curl myself into a ball and fall asleep before I have time to wonder if I will be able to.

chapter three

Someone is calling my name. Light streams through my tent. "Miho! Where are you?" the voice—my favorite voice—calls again.

"I'm here!" I call back, too woozy to sit up. I'm nauseous. I stare up at the ceiling wondering where I found a tent. Then I remember. The banner. The ad on it is facing me. Giant letters read ANYTHING IS POSSIBLE®. I'm sure it's some kind of self-improvement cult banner or something, but right now I think, *Yep,* anything, *including your boyfriend of two years having a kid with someone else at the ripe old age of eighteen, is possible.* I want to tear the banner into tiny pieces, but it's vinyl, so I throw it onto the sand. No point arguing with a banner.

I sit up and groan, holding my head so I don't do a face-plant into the sand. Blood pounds in my ears. Every muscle in my body hurts. It finally occurs to me: Did I drink any water at all last night? Eat anything? I'm dehydrated and I'm starving and I smell like the gross old gym lockers at school.

X is a few yards away. He walked right past me. He looks over and does a double take.

"Jeez, Miho. I thought that was a drunk or something under there." He takes off his school shoes, rolls up his uniform pants, and makes his way over to me in the sand. It's the same uniform that two-timing rat fink wears. He sits down on the bench. "Okay, spill," he says. My lip quivers.

"He's getting married," I say, or rather sob.

"Who?"

"Who do you think?"

"You don't mean—"

"I don't want to hear his name ever again," I say, cutting him off. "Even his name hurts."

"Oh my god," X says, pulling out his phone. I know he's texting everyone. Maybe I should have sent a group text, but in every group, there are little suballiances: the people you go to for certain things. I love all my friends, but I knew I wanted X: his shoulder to cry on, his sympathy, his fury on my behalf. X understands heartbreak. He slides his phone away into his satchel.

"How did you find out?" he asks. "I saw you before school yesterday and everything was fine. I saw him at school and he seemed totally normal."

"He broke it off. Just, out of the blue. We met up after school and he broke up with me."

"For no reason?"

"No, he told me the reason. But not the whole reason."

X waits. I try to fit the rage into sentences that go in chronological order, rather than letting loose the tornado of discoveries within me. Where do I even start?

"Okay," I say. "You remember I told you he used to date that girl at St. Agatha's? The one he broke up with when she went to study abroad in Japan for sophomore year?"

He nods.

"Well, what he told me yesterday was that he'd done something stupid, gotten drunk at a Christmas party they were both at, and he got her pregnant."

"What a piece of human garbage."

"I was real mad."

"Understatement?"

"Obviously. So he told me he was being *forced* to marry her, shotgun-wedding style, because she wants to keep it. And he said he didn't have the strength to see me anymore because he loved me too much to watch me go on without him, when he was being *trapped* into marrying her."

"I hope you slapped him."

"I didn't," I say sheepishly. "We did a whole 'last kiss' thing. It might have been the most romantic kiss of my entire life."

"With the guy who cheated on you."

"With the guy who cheated on me."

"Miho," X scolds, shaking his head.

"It seemed so Lancelot, you know?"

"Lancelot was a cheating piece of garbage too," X says.

"Exactly," I say. "Anyway, I said I understood, and that I was sorry and happy for him, but that I hoped we could be friends someday."

"So . . . okay."

"Because I *was* happy, you know? I was happy when I thought he cheated *once,* maybe because he was drunk, and was stepping up to deal with the consequences."

"You know that's messed up, right?"

Of course I know that's messed up. But I'm pretty sure *I* was a drunk mistake. I mean, I know I was a mistake, because my mom told me that all the time before she abandoned me, and I assume alcohol was involved because . . . well, my dad was involved. And even though my dad is great now, I wish it hadn't taken him ten years to step up and deal with the consequences. I wish it hadn't taken my mom abandoning me to make him man up and get his life together.

X knows exactly what I'm thinking, because he's my best friend. "Sorry, Mi," he says. "It's not messed up that you were happy. You're a good person for wishing them the best. But seriously. What a scumbag."

"Double seriously," I agree. "But that's not the story."

"Wait, what?"

"That's only half the story. Because in my heart I knew. I just *knew* it wasn't like that."

"And so—"

I sigh. My heart hurts even thinking of this.

"And so I looked her up. He was careful to never say her last name, but I knew where she went to school, a few things about her. And I found everything. A whole gallery of lies he told me. When he and I hooked up, she *was* studying in Japan, but I don't think he ever broke up with her. At least, she didn't think they were broken up. And then when she came back, he kept it up with both of us. Except apparently, she was his *real* girlfriend, the one who came to dinner with his parents, and I was on the down low."

"Oh, baby, *I* didn't know."

"Well, he's always been—"

"A very private person," X finishes for me, in a perfect imitation of that rat fink's smug, conceited, totally dialect-free voice. Even white people here have an accent, but he speaks the most non-Hawaiian English of any human on this island, like a Midwestern newscaster. When he heads to college, no one will even know he was born here.

X shakes his head in disbelief. "At school he mostly snobsplains. I don't think I've heard him say anything to another human being that didn't start with, 'Well, *actually* . . . ' I mean, not to be a jerk, but we put up with him mostly for your sake. He was a pretentious little cardboard snob just begging to get knocked down."

My face burns as X goes on.

"I particularly love how he holds out his books *just so* to make absolutely sure everyone can see the Very Important Dead White Men he was reading. Like, we get it. You've read Proust. When people like that are around *actual* smart people, you can see right through them. And it kind of makes you cringe. He was fun, and he was cute, but god, didn't you just hate him sometimes?"

No, I think. No I didn't.

I know X is trying to make me feel better, the same way I've deconstructed every single football-loving dimwit who wouldn't give him the time of day. I know he would never, ever think those things about me. But that's because he's my friend. You never think those things about your friends. But if my ex-boyfriend was so obviously a poser, then what am I?

"I'm not blaming you for not reading his mind," I say.

"I still feel bad," X says. "So you found out, and then what?"

"I was pissed. So I rode my bike to his house, and I tried to calm myself down, and I walked right up to his door. But when I got there, I saw her sitting on the porch. He must have been inside."

"And?"

"And I was going to walk up to him and tell him what I thought of him, right in front of her. I came up to the door. I said, 'I'm Miho.' And . . . she had no clue. She had *no clue* who I was."

X squints questioningly. "How do you know?"

"She asked if I was delivering something."

"Wow. Stuck-up."

"To be fair, my bike rack does say 'pizza' on it."

"Even so. You'd think she would have seen someone our age and thought 'a friend' and not 'a service worker.' "

"Why would she? I honestly don't think he ever mentioned me. Not once. Girls remember things like that."

"So you told her?"

I pause.

"You *didn't tell her*?" X whisper-shouts. "Why? Why not out him?"

"I was in shock," I say defensively. "It never occurred to me that anyone could tell a lie this big."

"So what did you do?"

"I said I must be at the wrong house for my imaginary delivery and rode off."

"And that was that?"

"That was that. Except for the series of increasingly furious voice mails and text messages I sent him. But he hasn't responded. So I guess that was that."

We're quiet then. The only thing I hear is my stomach growling.

"Thanks for getting me," I say at last.

"You should have called last night."

"I was busy."

"With what?"

"Pyrotechnics."

He snorts. "Drama queen."

"Closet queen."

"Meanie," he says, but he's laughing. "So what do you want to do?"

"Curl up here and die in your arms."

"Yes to the first part, no to the second."

"Fine," I say. I lie down and put my head in his lap. I'm so tired. X leans forward, looking me over, looking all around.

"Miho," he says slowly. "Where are your shoes?"

The rest of our crew shows up one by one. While I was dozing, X texted them the basics.

Lani is first, because she tries to hit the breakfast crowd before school in her food truck. She pulls up on her scooter, slides onto the bench, and puts my feet in her lap. I hear the faint click of the beads braided into her cornrows when she moves. Out of the corner of my eye, I see her mouthing "Shoes?" to X. He shrugs. She hands a breakfast sandwich to X, who greedily unwraps it. Crumbs start falling on my face, but I don't move. Lani tries to hand me a sandwich, but I shake my head. I was starving a minute ago, but now I'm horribly nauseous. Lani hands something in a thermos to me, but even the idea of putting something in my mouth makes me queasy.

"Drink it, Miho," Lani orders.

I sit up. Lani has been my friend since the first day of middle school, when she and her best friend, Trin, let me sit at their table. A group of boys made up a song called, "Fat Girl, Nerd Girl, New Girl" that fall and serenaded us with it every day at lunch for weeks. I didn't mind: I'd been the new girl before. But Trinity—"Nerd Girl"—may or may not have very shortly thereafter caused "severe testicular trauma" to one of those boys, coincidentally at the same time that Lani spilled her milk on the monitor. I didn't see anything. No one did.

Lani is our "Mom" friend. So I don't make her tell me twice. Once I start drinking—pineapple sweet tea, her newest hit—I can't stop, even though it's too cold. My brain knows I need to slow down, pace myself, but my body is so thirsty that I can't make myself take the bottle away from my lips.

I drop the empty thermos into the sand, my eyes squeezed shut.

"Are you okay?" Lani asks me. "Are you crying?"

I shake my head again. "Brain freeze," I tell her.

Trinity arrives next, mysteriously on foot. We never know how Trin gets around. She magically appears places, transported by an extended network of brothers and cousins, motorcycles and trucks. Hawaiian Muni, I think of it. Trinity slides onto the bench between me and Lani. X shouts as we almost push him off. There's barely room for the four of us.

"I'm sorry," she says. She reaches out to me, and I instinctively throw my arms up to block the punch. She rolls her eyes, insulted. "It was a hug." Then she punches me in the shoulder. "For flinching," she clarifies.

Trin takes her breakfast from Lani, stuffing it into her mouth like the garbage disposal she is. "So it's, like, *official*?" Trin asks with her mouth full.

"She's knitting baby socks on Instagram," I say.

"She might miscarry," Trinity says. "Why exactly are they going through with it?"

"With what?"

"The baby."

"The baby is non-optional for some people," I explain. "She is one of those people."

"It's weird that they're not trying to hide it until after they're married, then," Trinity says. "Isn't that what you're supposed to do if you get knocked up? Get married real fast and hide it?"

"No one is ever fooled by that," Lani says, pointing to herself, a not-quite-in-wedlock baby. "Besides, she looks like a bridezilla. She probably wants flowers and a cake and a bridal shower and all that, even though everyone knows this is a major screwup."

"But then, if she miscarries, does it get called off?" Trinity asks.

"It doesn't matter now," I say. I know that this is what I am supposed to feel, so I add: "He's a cheater, and he lied to me for two years. Why would I want him back? He's dead to me."

"I'm glad," Trinity says with her mouth full again, another paper wrapper in her lap. Did she steal my sandwich? I look in panic at Lani, who laughs. Two. She brought Trin two. Playing favorites, the jerk. But then Lani hands me my very own, and we're golden.

"I'm glad too," Lani says. "He was such a pretentious waste of oxygen."

X nods in agreement. "I mean honestly, who wears a Harris tweed blazer in Hawai'i?"

"I mean honestly, who can point out Harris tweed?" Rei asks from behind us. We all turn around. She strides up, looking like a living Anthropologie catalog. Her boyfriend, Wyatt, is hanging back by her whisper-silent silver Prius. Rei puts her arms around me from behind the bench and kisses the top of my head. X pulls me onto his lap so that Rei can sit down.

Lani leans over the back of the bench and gestures to Wyatt, food in hand, like she's trying to lure in a scared dog. Wyatt and Rei haven't been dating that long. He's always a little awkward, and a little afraid of us. Understandably.

"Hey," Wyatt says. "Sorry about—"

"Don't say his name," I shout, covering my ears. "I never want to hear it ever again."

"Okay," Wyatt says. He sits on the sand, observing from a distance.

"I can't believe she's cheating with your boyfriend," Rei says. "What about the girl code?"

Rei's a big believer in the "girl code." In middle school, Rei was my dance partner in PE because there were more girls than boys. She was a good sport about it, even though it meant she didn't get to dance with the coolest boy in school, who clearly wanted to dance with her. "Sisters before misters," she says whenever it comes up.

"Technically, I'm cheating with her boyfriend," I clarify. "She came first. I'm the side chick. I just didn't know it."

"I still think you should tell her," X says.

"I don't even know where she lives."

"X could find out," Trin says. "Hell, I could find out. Give me two seconds—"

"No," I cut them off. "It won't fix anything."

"Not for you. But maybe for her," Rei says. "I'd tell her because I'd want to know myself. When she finds out—and she *will* find out because a cheater is a cheater—she's going to feel like everyone in the universe is laughing at her. It will hurt way worse later on."

Lani nods. "Think of my mom. That's what my dad did to her. Same deal: rushed wedding, baby on the way. Think of finding that out when you're in your thirties. At thirty you're basically dead, guys. Dead. Your life is over. I can't even imagine being thirty. Imagine finding out that the father of your kids has been screwing around with other girls since before you got married. That every time he picks up his phone or uses a computer, it's to cheat on you. My mom took my dad's cricket bat and smashed our home computer into computer salad. Every once in a while I still find microchip bits under the furniture. But then she didn't get off the couch for two whole years, and now I think she's addicted to her Prozac. You could save this dumb girl from that before it's too late."

I know they're right, but my mouth goes dry because I'm not thinking of her as Lani's mom, I'm thinking of her baby as me. And when I think of it that way, I just can't.

"Good lord, two years?" Trinity says after the silence gets too long. "Men don't have enough balls you could possibly kick to make that right."

"I beg to differ," Wyatt says. "Maybe repeat applications would be required."

"I mean, what can you even do to get back at a guy for that?"

"Same thing he did to me," I say. *"Damnatio memoriae."*

X rolls his eyes, grinning at me. "Show-off. What does that mean?"

"Erase him. Forget him. Strike his name from history."

My friends consider the idea. "I like it," Rei says at last. "The worst punishment is to be forgotten. And he deserves it. I mean, what a scumbag."

"He's not even a bag of scum. He's a full bucket," Lani says.

"Oh, I like that," Trinity says. "That should be his name now, if we're really striking it. Scumbucket."

"God, that's perfect," Rei says, laughing. She stands. She plays a pretend trumpet, then unrolls a mimed scroll. "Hear ye, hear ye, the cheating piece of garbage formerly playing the role of Miho's Boyfriend is to be known henceforth as Scumbucket."

My friends cheer.

"What say you, my lady?" Rei asks. "Yea or nay?"

"Yea," I say. They cheer again.

Scumbucket. I play with it in my head. I love it, because *Scumbucket* loved naming things. My bike was Balius, though I never called it that. Secretly, I never thought my bike needed a name. It'd be like naming my hand. His car was Xanthus. I let him pick my dog's name. He even named his junk. He called it Byron.

Scumbucket. I name *him* for once.

As though by telepathic consensus, we all turn to the ocean.

How can anywhere on our planet hold this much color and light?

I forget, for a second, that we're all standing here because a boy took my heart and stomped on it.

"God, what a Friday," Lani says. "I can't believe this all happened yesterday. In just one day!"

"One day can change everything," I say. "It's terrifying. Anything is possible."

chapter four

There are no trailer parks in Hawai'i. They rust, and the wind hates them, and people think they're ugly. Apparently, it doesn't matter how many people are homeless so long as you never have to see a trailer from your five-million-dollar windows.

Where I live is the closest spiritual equivalent to a trailer park, so that's what we call it. The Trailer Park. Dad and his three best friends planned it this way: that they'd all get old living off the grid in these "definitely not a trailer" houses in Hawai'i, away from all the mistakes they made on the mainland. Of course, they didn't plan on me.

This morning my friends split up into different cars at the beach: Lani and Trin, Rei and Wyatt, me and X. X dropped me off on his way to school. He's missing the bell for sure, but it's spring semester of senior year, and everyone I know is a shoo-in for their dream schools. X got a full ride at Cornell.

Rei got her Juilliard acceptance last week, which is tragically far from Wyatt at Stanford—early admission, he's known since November. Lani will probably go to UH Hilo as a cover for expanding her food truck business because her mom has no imagination. Trinity is headed to MIT, but will be biting her nails until she gets the letter. The school literally paid for her to visit during some diversity outreach program, where they ship in a bunch of minority kids they want to apply. They wine and dine—well, pop and pizza—them for a whole week. They show them all the cool labs, get them talking to current students, sell them on it. She's obviously getting in. She got to see snow in Boston. It was the first time she'd ever seen snow and it blew her mind. She's the first person in generations of her family to leave Hawai'i, even for vacation. All my friends are outliers and prodigies. Even Scumbucket got into his dream school: a tiny college called Reed in Oregon. He was planning on taking a gap year to backpack around Europe. Now he'll spend it drowning in diapers.

I'm the only one without a plan or a future.

I stomp up the drive to the cluster of four tiny houses, each a different color. Mine is the purple one on the end. In the big clearing in front of the houses, our three neighbors are in their usual place. Mr. Bu and Mr. Kalani are sitting on overturned buckets with Mr. Oshiro, staring down at the game of Go. They are all drinking beer. It's eight a.m.

Mr. Oshiro reaches over Mr. Bu's shoulder. Mr. Bu swats his hand away.

Mr. Oshiro sighs. "But you could—"

"If you want to play, you are more than welcome," says Mr. Bu.

"Why can't we play checkers?" asks Mr. Kalani.

"Because Go is a game of elegance and strategy, and checkers is a game played by kindergartners you must entertain at family reunions," Mr. Oshiro snaps. "You could learn Go if you only tried."

"Did I lose?" Mr. Kalani asks.

"You both lost and you're both too stupid to see it," Mr. Oshiro says with a sigh. He notices me and smiles. Then he looks at his watch. I sprint past them before he can ask me why I'm not in school. I'm winded when I get there and almost trip over the minefield of slippers and shoes outside the door.

"Miho?" Dad asks. He is scrubbing the sink. He likes things clean.

I knew I'd have to face him. There's no sneaking around in this house. The whole layout is a straight shot back down one hall: kitchen, living room, Dad's bedroom, bathroom, my bedroom. A trailer without wheels. The houses in the Trailer Park are identical. In the others, my neighbors have hobbies at the end of their hallways. Mr. Bu has his workshop, Mr. Kalani his sumi-e painting, Mr. Oshiro his bizarre conspiracy-theory geographical monitoring system that makes me wonder if he is slightly unhinged. I don't know what Dad originally had at the end of his hall, because by the time I got there, it was all set up for me.

Achilles comes out and yips hello at me, bouncing off the

walls. Even my tripod dog has two up on my monopod dad who has his old battered plastic leg on, the one with the huge crack in it that he literally duct-taped back together, paired with his hideous dad shorts. He has a much nicer leg and many pairs of inoffensive shorts, but god forbid he ever wear them.

"Silence, Aki-chan," he snaps at Achilles. "Miho, you should be in school."

"It was a rough night."

"I gathered. You should be in school."

"I'm sick," I say.

"What happened?"

"Don't ask me."

"I've already asked you. And you need to answer me," he says. I sit down on the tiny loveseat. Our house isn't big enough for a couch.

"I got my heart broke," I say.

"What happened with—"

"His name is Scumbucket now," I interrupt. Dad stops cleaning and turns around to look at me.

"What?" he asks. His yellow gloves squeak as he crosses his arms.

"Trinity came up with it. I never want to hear his name again. I am striking him from the record."

"Because?"

"Reasons," I say, not sure I want to tell him. "He broke up with me."

"I'm sorry, Miho. But you still have to go to school."

"Seriously?"

"Seriously."

"Dad. He's been dating someone else the whole time we were together."

"Even so. School."

"He got her pregnant. He's marrying her."

"And I believe that you can consider the lesson there from your seat in class."

I stare at him, narrow my eyes. He narrows his right back.

"Do you not have one word of sympathy for your heart-broken offspring?"

"Miho. I love you. When you hurt, I hurt. But this is not the end of the world, and you must go to school. Think about your college applications."

"I'm not going to college."

"You got a sixteen hundred on your SAT. We all know you're going to college, you stubborn mule of a child. And when you go back to your teachers for college recommendations, when colleges look at your grades, they need to see that you are as exceptional on paper as I know you are."

I groan and cover my face with a pillow. We've been going back and forth about this for about a year now. My dad didn't go to college. He says I'm too smart not to. I say we're too poor for me to go. He says X got a full ride to Cornell. I say X is going to be a Silicon Valley billionaire, and my number one marketable skill is delivering pizzas on a bike. He says art is just as important as computers. Him: loans. Me: debt. Him: investment. Me: waste. He keeps saying, "You won't even try," like I'm lazy or something. He doesn't get it.

"Time heals all wounds," he says. "I bet you can still make second period." He reaches for his keys with the gloves still on.

"God, could you pretend that my feelings matter for one second? The great romance of my life has ended. Have a heart."

"I know you are too smart to believe that. Maybe this is a good lesson for you. Maybe next time you will listen before you involve yourself with . . . a Scumbucket."

I engage in another eye-narrowing.

"Hindsight's twenty-twenty. You only said that he was pretentious. You didn't say that he was a Scumbucket."

"You will recall, I also said that he seemed untrustworthy. That he wasn't treating you like you deserve to be treated."

"That's just what all dads say."

"All dads are right. A man who won't introduce you to his friends, his parents, let you be a part of his life except in some video game or on a phone . . . he is not trustworthy. And now you know."

"Yeah," I say. "Now I know."

Dad sighs.

"You can be sick today, Miho, and I will call your school. But come Monday, you are going back to class, and don't think you're getting off easy with last night's escapades either. You smell like drugs."

"Yeah, yeah," I say, even though I do not smell like drugs. I smell like burned shoes. "I mean, our neighbors are getting tipsy on the lawn at eight in the morning like they do *every single day*, but I spend a night on wholesome vigorous exercise and I'm the delinquent."

"You better not be smoking drugs."

"Send in the drug dog if you don't believe me," I say, pointing to Achilles, who couldn't find a steak smack in the middle of the kitchen floor. "It's bike stink."

"Don't you lie to me."

"Never," I say, heading to my room. I do stink.

"Miho?" he calls after me. I turn around. "I *am* sorry. I know you cared about him a lot."

"I loved him, Dad. I thought he loved me."

"I know, my flower. Sleep it off."

chapter five

I wake up before the sun rises on Saturday morning, and it's all still true. I tell myself not to think about him, swear up and down that he's not going to take one more day of my life. The drama is done. He's a jerk and I'm over it. Completely. Who even cares.

I look at my phone. It's full of messages from my friends, most of which are Scumbucket hot takes: what a pretentious douchebag he is, how his dick is tiny, how he'll probably go bald. That's nothing on the shade they have cultivated for *her*. My phone is getting blown up with the Shade Olympics. She's basic, she's a J. Crew jock, an airhead, and my personal favorite, she "looks like an ugly mushroom." The crew has texted several convincing examples of fungal specimens. I can see the resemblance. I join in: "Fail that is a cute mushroom."

Trin hits back in a minute: "That mushroom kills people."

"Confirmed by Eagle Scout," Wyatt adds. "Do not apply mouth to shroom."

"Too late," Rei chimes in. "RIP Scumbucket."

I laugh. I can think of a million catty comments to add, but the worst thing I can think of, I didn't come up with myself. It's something Scumbucket said about her whenever she came up.

He and I had this running joke, that he was a wandering monk and she was his walking hair shirt. His *penance.* After school he'd text me, "Starbucks with the Shirt. So basic." Or, "At the Shirt's race sherpa-ing all her basic Shirt stuff." Or, "Shopping with the Shirt please kill me."

At the time, I thought it was cool how he was nice to her, even if he whined about it behind her back. Being nice to your ex seems like a good thing. I should have known. She was never his Shirt. I mean, maybe *I'm* the Shirt. I get it now. Guys who are mean like that, they're never mean about just one girl. They're dicks across the board. You think you're the exception. You never are.

I decide not to tell my friends about the Shirt thing, even though it's hilarious.

The truth is, I don't see how she could possibly be a Shirt. She studied abroad in Japan and she speaks good Japanese. Despite my name, I've never been, and I know basically no Japanese or anything about Japan, except for a few family dishes I learned from Dad. She also speaks Hawaiian, and her *halau* performed at the Merrie Monarch Festival and won some kind of award. I only remember the words you hear all the time, like *ono, aloha, mahalo,* and the correct pronunciation of "ukulele." Forget about the dancing. Not even if my life depended on it.

She's somehow better at being both Japanese and Hawaiian than me, even though she's dyeing her red hair black. And I know that's not true—she'll always be a white girl pretending to be those things—but like, if you asked a Japanese person if I'm Japanese, or a Hawaiian person if I'm Hawaiian, or a Black person if I'm Black . . . chances are, they'd tell you no. So am I any better because I'm at least part Japanese? For sure she's beating me at pretending, at the very least.

It gets weirder with her too. She loves her bike exactly like I love my bike. Her ride is a sweet pink Cervélo, and mine's an intermittently mobile garbage heap I found on Craigslist. She probably spends as much time on it as I do, though not for deliveries.

The problem with trying to hate people is, if you look too closely, you usually find a lot to like. I wish I could hate her. But she's too much like me. Except, you know, better. Like she's the brand name, and I'm the crappy store brand no one actually wants.

My eyes burn with tears. I don't know why. I should be laughing. No, I should be *angry.* He doesn't deserve to make me sad.

I take a deep breath. Do something. Stay busy. Then I'll forget him. I'll ghost him right back. *Damnatio memoriae.*

I don't even look at my room, the mess I made gathering up every single thing that reminds me of him. I get up. I put my headphones on. I leave.

I spend Saturday morning on basic necessities. I make a list. I borrow Dad's pickup truck to go get my bike, then spend all morning fixing it. Mr. Bu lends me his tools and attempts to lend me his advice. Something about "finding centeredness" and meditation healing a broken heart. He invites me to come sit zazen with him at his temple. I politely decline. I can imagine literally nothing worse than sitting silently with these thoughts. Hard no. I want to bike as far away from them as I can.

I pick up groceries. I weed the garden. I wash the windows. I do the laundry. I get all the way into next week's chores. I make lunch for Dad and the neighbors, and we all eat it on overturned buckets around the lawn table. My neighbors are drinking beer, except Dad, because he's a reformed alcoholic. I like their conversations, which spiral off in all directions, taking me far away.

Finally, *finally,* it's time for work.

I bike over to Uncle Tua's slowly, watching the world go by. I like to look at other people's houses, and delivering pizzas, I get to see into a lot of doorways. I hate waiting tables, though. People don't see waiters. They expect you to be invisible or, if they're the bad kind of tourist, to be a parody of Hawai'i. Occasionally, if the punters are sufficiently drunk, they make racists remarks about "babes in grass skirts and coconut bras." Once when I was fifteen, a guy said that and grabbed my butt, and Uncle Tua beat the living daylights out of him in the parking lot. Uncle Tua is not really my uncle; he's everyone's uncle—he just particularly likes me.

Pizza is my favorite thing, after my dog and my bike and

painting. I could work at Uncle Tua's forever, honestly. I love the food, for one. And I like the way everything happens the same way every day, with little changes. The changes seem manageable, different views out the same windows in my day. I'm perfectly still in a world full of people rushing to and fro. It's very zen.

"Delivery already," Tua says as I coast in toward the outdoor pizza oven. He's got his apron on, and he's watching the television news on a smoke-stained old TV. I glance inside. It's packed. "Want me to send one of the boys in a car?" Tua says. He doesn't actually say that, but it's what I hear. What he says exchanges some prepositions, adds in a few yeahs.

"Miho. Earth to Miho."

"Sorry. I got it. Can you clock me in?" I say.

"I pay you. You think I don't remember?"

"You pay me too much every time."

"Subjective accounting."

"I know you're a money launderer, Uncle Tua."

"Get going. Pizza's getting cold."

Without getting off, I swing my leg over so I'm balancing on one side of the bike. Tua calls this my "circus move" and he always cheers, even though he's seen me do it a zillion times. I circle around so the rack is facing him, put my foot down while he bungee-cords three pizzas to the back in their padded case. He hands me an address and I don't even have to look it up. It's close. I know the street. I can make it in ten minutes if I push hard. It doesn't improve the tips. I still like the challenge.

"Gonna be a busy night. You ready to race?"

"Always."

"I'll make your specialty to take home later. Be quick." (He says, "Go fast kine.")

"No other way to go."

And then I'm off, pedaling hard. It's the best part of my job.

~

After work, I walk alongside my bike on my way home. I have an open box of pizza bungee-corded to the back—my shift freebie—and I eat slice after slice with my free hand as I hobble along. My legs are *killing* me. As long as I kept biking, I was fine, but now that I'm walking, I feel like my legs might give out. Every few steps my knee jumps forward as the muscles in the front of my leg betray me. I'm basically using my bike as a crutch.

Even worse, I have gnarly saddle sores. My butt is on fire, like right where butt becomes leg. Every once in a while I get this on a busy night. I may be the top teen consumer of off-brand Desitin. So embarrassing, but it works.

Still. Nothing tastes as good as this pizza does right now, I have 140 dollars in tips zipped into my pocket, thick as a brick, and the air has that amazing ominous electricity that always happens right before a storm.

What an awesome night. Even the hurting is awesome. I can feel it in my lungs, in my heart. I feel . . . happy.

"Miho!" It's a voice from across the street. My heart jumps in my chest. I look up, look around. "Hey!" the voice shouts again. This time I spot him. Wyatt.

My brain is playing tricks on me. Wyatt doesn't sound a thing like Scumbucket.

"What are you doing out so late?" I ask as he jogs across the street to me. He gestures to his backpack. Swim stuff. Wyatt is one of those nerdy swim kids with two hundred plastic meet tags hanging off a dripping bag, shaved legs, and goggle rings around his eyes. At the beach he wears normal shorts, but at the pool he wears tiny lady-style bikini bottoms and is totally casual about it. Doofus. Even so, he kind of looks like a K-Pop idol in his post-swim tracksuit. Almost pulls it off.

"Where are you headed?" he asks.

"Home. You?"

"Home."

"Cool," I say. He smiles.

We walk in silence for about thirty seconds before it's too awkward.

"Want some pizza?" I nod to the open box.

"Sure," he says, taking a piece. "This why you're walking your bike?"

I scoff. "Please. I can totally eat pizza and ride a bike."

"Why are you walking, then? You a mobile restaurant now? Tua's bike food cart?"

"I leave that to Lani." I'm too proud to admit I'm sore, so I say, "I felt like walking. Nice night."

"Wish you were a restaurant. I get so hungry after I swim. Like, eat-a-whole-pizza hungry."

"I . . . did not eat all that," I lie, looking into the box at the solitary slice left. I totally did. Very unladylike.

"Oh, for sure deserved," he says, holding his hands up. "No judgment. Didn't you ride over a hundred miles yesterday?"

"Yeah," I say with a smile.

"That's bananapants. I'm starving from an hour in the pool." *Bananapants.* I smile. Who says that?

"Why are you swimming so late?"

He shrugs. "Helps me think."

"I get that," I say. He swallows, eyes me nervously.

"Hey, so, Rei filled me in on the whole Scumbucket saga, and I . . ." He trails off. "I didn't get it on Friday. I didn't get how awful what he did was."

"It's fine," I say as breezily as I can. Good lord, this can't be the thing that breaks me, not in front of Rei's boyfriend of all people. But I sense the prickles of tears. I force them down, walk a little ahead of him so he can't see. My legs hurt. I slow down.

Wyatt clears his throat as we come up even again. "I know we're all focused on the whole Scumbucket thing, but real talk, how is it possible that you are even standing right now? A hundred miles? Seriously?"

I grin, even though I know that he's only trying to change the subject so I won't cry. "As the banner says, anything is possible."

"What banner?"

"Oh, some stupid banner I found on the beach. I used it as a tent last night."

"And it said 'Anything is possible'?"

"Yup. Bright red letters. Felt like a sign. I mean, it was a sign, but it also *felt* like a sign. Don't you love the poetry of the universe?"

"That's the Ironman slogan," Wyatt says. "Did it have a little *M* with a dot?" He draws it in the air.

"Yeah," I say, thinking back. "What is that again? Like a race or something?"

"It's a triathlon. You swim 2.4 miles, bike 112 miles, and run 26.2 miles. 140.6 miles. It was invented right here. Well, in Honolulu."

"Triathlons are from Hawai'i?" I ask, incredulous. I reach for the last piece of pizza, and I see the ravenous look on Wyatt's face. "Split it?"

"Oh thank god," he says. "Hold up. I know you can eat and bike and probably spin plates while you're at it, but I don't think I can do this in motion."

We pause as he tears the slice of pizza in two. It's weird, standing on either side of my bike so close. This is the first time Wyatt and I have ever talked without Rei.

"So you were saying? About triathlons?"

"Oh right," he says with his mouth full. We start walking again. "No, they're not from Hawai'i. But the first Ironman was held in Honolulu. These crazy people were arguing about whether swimmers, cyclists, or runners were the fittest."

"Cyclists, obviously."

"Swimmers," he jabs back. Then he thinks, and raises his nerd finger that he always puts up as he thinks through a problem. "Well, *actually,* it depends on how you define the problem—"

"But the race?"

"Right, the race. So they came up with a race that combined the Waikiki Roughwater Swim, this bike race that used to go all the way around the island, and the Honolulu marathon. And that's how the world got Ironman. And it got bigger and bigger, year after year."

"How do you know all that?"

He shrugs. "You can always spot the triathletes at the pool. And I don't mean that in a good way."

"How?"

"Race caps. Branded bags. Tan lines here and here"—he points to his thigh and the middle of his arm—"giant egos to match giant legs. Rude as hell to rec swimmers and kids. Insist on swimming in the fastest lane. And the joke is, the guys like that are all mediocre swimmers. At least, compared to actual swimmers."

I laugh. "Well, that's just lunacy. 140.6 miles? That's not even possible."

But then it clicks. 140.6.

Where have I seen that number before?

On her Instagram account. *Ironman.* She was training for an Ironman race before she got knocked up. It was all over her account. #imtraining: not hashtag "I'm training" but hashtag "IM training": *Ironman* training.

My heart lurches. Maybe anything is possible for her.

"Actually," Wyatt says, holding up his nerd finger. "The bike is like half the race. A lot of people call it a bike race with a swim warm-up and a marathon for a cooldown."

"A marathon is not a cooldown."

"You probably did half that last night after your ride."

"Walking."

Wyatt smirks. "I mean, in theory it's a run. In practice it's more of a jog and shuffle-o'-shame for most people. So yeah, it definitely is possible."

Hashtag Swim Bike Run. He's right, I could totally do the bike part. And I swim all the time, even though it's not laps. I'm notorious for refusing to run even in gym class, but if I could walk—

I cut off my thoughts.

I wish I was that person. The brand-name version of me. But people who ride delivery bikes don't do triathlons. People on pink Cervélos do. That's just how it is.

"You okay?" Wyatt asks.

"Yeah."

"This is my turnoff," he says. I realize he's headed for a not-particularly-nice part of town. For some reason I thought he lived in Rei's swanky hood. "You sure you're okay?"

"Totally," I say. "Gonna bike the rest of the way."

I snap on my helmet and put one foot on the pedal to push off, then go to swing my leg over like a show-off, but my muscles are trashed. I mistime it trying to get my body to cooperate, and the bike starts falling sideways. Before I hit the ground,

Wyatt has dropped his bag and caught me. We are standing, my bike tipped halfway out from under me, him holding me up like the Leaning Tower of Pisa, completely ridiculous.

I put my foot down and get off my bike, and we both start laughing.

"On second thought, maybe I'll go with the shuffle-o'-shame," I say.

"Whatever gets you across the finish line. You sure you're good?"

"My pride took the brunt of the fall."

"May that always be the case." He turns onto his street.

"See you round, swim nerd."

"Later, bike nerd."

chapter six

I wake up on Sunday morning at four a.m. I haven't been asleep, but at four a.m. I officially accept my lack of sleep as wakefulness.

I lie in bed feeling sorry for myself until 4:15. *Get ahold of yourself,* I think. *Get out of bed.* I start to pull out my painting supplies but stop. The case where I keep my art stuff under my bed is open. I look at the wall where I threw brushes, tubes of oil paint, my watercolors, a few canvases, one with a giant hole where I stomped my foot right through it.

I bite my lip. My heart sinks. I've been staying so busy that I totally forgot I did that.

I gather up the paint and brushes from the floor. It was mostly drama; nothing but that canvas is hurt. I hold it out in front of me.

Wheatfield with Crows.

I painted it. It's only a copy. It is not even as good as a good copy of the original. But it's mine. I made it. Van Gogh made copies too, as he tried to find his way. Copies help you understand the world of another person.

I kept it secret for a long time, hidden under my bed. I'm normally not shy about art stuff—our whole house is plastered with pictures I've drawn, each carefully framed by Dad. But this one . . . was different. Somehow I knew that this was me admitting what I really wanted: to be an artist. Like that's something you can just *be.*

The one person I ever showed it to was Scumbucket.

Lots of people love Van Gogh. I know that. It's not exactly a deep cut. But Scumbucket held it up and got a look on his face I had never seen before. Not a cynical one. He had a lot of those. He was sad. He told me he'd seen it in Amsterdam. He said it was the only time he'd ever cried in front of a piece of art.

"I would love to see it for real," I told him, looking at my imitation. He told me that I didn't need to because I already understood what Van Gogh was trying to say, but that he needed more than anything to see it with me by his side. He told me that he had never met someone who could put into colors and lines what he saw when he looked at those colors and lines.

We were supposed to go to Amsterdam this summer. We were going to leave on my birthday. We had "The Itinerary." It was all set.

I look at my painting. He doesn't own this. I might not be able to fix it, but I promise myself I won't throw it away. I shove it back under my bed.

Painting is too much of a mess. No reading because half my books are ashes on the beach now. No video games because . . .

I look at my PlayStation.

It's his old PlayStation. I totally forgot.

He bought me *Moonslaught,* the fourth *Eldritch Codex* game, when it came out last year. He knew I couldn't afford it and he wanted us to spend time together there since we usually only saw each other in real life once a week or so. He wanted us to be together in *Themria.* Now I know why. It's because he wouldn't get caught.

I tell myself not to do the thing I am currently doing, but my hands don't listen as the creepy loading screen greets me with the circle of invented runes. I only have two allies, and I can see right away that the last time Scumbucket was on was Wednesday, when we met up for a few hours to run around and ride horses. He said he loved me, and it was so weird to be looking at his avatar and for him to say that. He hasn't been on since.

I shut it down. Stupid. What was I even hoping for?

I look around my room. My heart is pounding for no good reason. I try not to think of him, but everything in my room reminds me of him, and looking at my phone, I want to text him and beg him to tell me it isn't true and tell me that he loves me and that I matter. What is he doing right now? What are *they* doing right now? What if, if I had texted him exactly the right thing, at exactly the right moment, none of this would ever have happened and he would have dumped her instead? If I wait, will he come back? If not to the real world, at least to *Themria*? What if it's not too late?

These thoughts are just heartbroken synapses firing in my brain. I know that. But I can't turn off this light show of sorrow and regret.

4:30. My god. Time has slowed down.

I try to shift my focus, but it's like how my legs kept giving out after my long ride. I just can't. When you go past your limit, your body fails. So does your heart.

I thought I could outrace this. Burn it on the beach. All I did was delay the inevitable.

I get back into bed. Tears roll down my face as I let every bad thing I've been forcing myself not to think roll over me. Worthless. Forgettable. Stupid. Ugly. I cry until I can't cry anymore. Not angry tears, like that first night. Helpless tears.

4:45. It felt like it lasted ages, the way crying always does. I roll over in bed with a hiccup. I turn on the television and pull my *Thin Man* movies off the shelf. X pirated them all for me and burned them onto DVDs. I put the first one in and get back under the covers.

X and I watched one of these movies each night over the first week we became friends. Since then, we've watched them five or six times apiece in the background while we do our homework, texted each other the best lines in gifs hundreds more. I know every frame. They star William Powell as Nick Charles, a detective, and Myrna Loy as Nora Charles, his rich wife and partner in crime. X loved these movies because they're how he wished the world could be, all glamour and witty banter. I loved all that too, but for me, it was all about the spark between Nick and Nora. I loved how two people could fit together like that: partners in crime.

When Scumbucket and I hooked up, I made him watch them, and he got it. We were kind of like them, but backward: Nora is rich and Nick is working-class. It became our thing, playing Nick and Nora. At least, I thought it was. We watched all of them straight through in a row once. It was right when we started *really* dating. He was housesitting for the parents of one of his rich friends, and we had the pool house of this mini mansion to ourselves. It took us sixteen hours and twelve minutes because we kept putting the movie on pause to "chill."

I remember kissing him goodbye at the gate at dawn. The colors of that sunrise found their way into everything I painted for a month. I remember running through the side yard, marveling at a tacky lit-up fountain with a Buddha statue on it. How much did it cost to run that thing? But for once I wasn't put off by it. I felt like I had won the universe because I had *him,* and I loved *him* and we were perfect.

Stupid. Stupid. Stupid.

Right now, these movies are ruined. They'll never be the same, and neither will Van Gogh, or anything else I shared with him. So many of my favorite things have his fingerprints on them because I trusted him to hold them.

But I watch all six movies anyway.

It takes me eleven hours and fourteen minutes, including breaks for sobbing into my pillow. Dad comes into my room a few times. He says nothing. I'm grateful. He brings me Thai curry manapua and a blue Slurpee from the 7-Eleven. The food does make me feel a little better. Achilles curls up next to me, ready to protect me from a threat he doesn't understand. It's the best thing ever when your dumbbell dog has your back.

As the last film closes, I force myself to sit up. I turn off the television and try to stand. Not even six. Too early to go to sleep.

I pull out my phone, which is full of messages from my friends asking if I'm okay. X texted me four hours ago: "Come out tonight."

I don't even wash my face. I just leave.

chapter seven

We always meet on a beach close to Rei's house on Sundays. It's usually pretty deserted. Every once in a while a family of tourists or a group of rowdy locals will drop by, but they're almost never rude to us. We started going there because someone close by didn't password-protect their Wi-Fi—thank you, owner of Charter_Spectrum11—and by the time they got wise to it, we had fallen into a routine. Now X and Trinity take turns cracking the Wi-Fi of the local mansions, and we mooch until our luck runs out.

I ride over, careful of my toes in slippers. By the time I pull up, I know coming out was the right thing. My friends are talking more than studying around a big picnic table, and I hang back and watch them for a second. They go quiet as I get off my bike. I must look awful.

"Hey, baby girl," Lani says, but she says it with this weird pity in her voice that makes me want to hide under a rock. It's obvious I've been crying all day.

"What are you guys up to?" I ask in my cheeriest voice.

Trin ticks off the circle, pointing: "Chem, history, Shakespeare, stats, and calc," she finishes, pointing to herself.

"How are you only in calculus?" X asks.

"We don't have super-calculus in public school," Trinity says.

"We also don't have your fancy lunches," Lani says.

"Or your massive theater program," Rei says.

"Or your cool uniforms," Wyatt adds. We all look at Wyatt. "I like wearing ties," he says sheepishly.

"You girls should all have gone to St. Agatha's." X pauses, knowing exactly what I'm thinking. *She* goes to St. Agatha's. We would have been classmates.

"The only reason X went to King's Prep is because our eighth-grade teacher, Mr. 'Bow Ties Are Cool' Bautista, went to bat for him," I tell Wyatt. "Mr. Bautista showed up at X's house and told his parents that they had a prodigy on their hands, and that if they didn't send him to King's Prep, they would be doing a disservice to humanity."

"Stop," X says, blushing.

"It's true," Rei says. "We're big fish in a public pond, but X is a legit prodigy."

"You're not big fish in a small pond, Rei," X says. "You're going to freaking Juilliard. And Wyatt, you're going to Stanford. Everyone at this table is a fish of unusual size."

"Well, except me," I say.

A silence falls.

"You just don't know what you want to do yet," Rei says eventually. "Your dad won't shut up about your SAT scores."

"If I hear the number sixteen hundred one more time, I'm going to lose it," Trinity says with a smile. "He thinks sixteen hundred is God's triumphant thumbprint on your forehead or something."

"It's impressive. You should be proud of yourself," Wyatt says.

I shrug.

"Please. Miho's always been a genius. Did you even study?" Trinity asks me. I shrug again. "See?"

It wouldn't be cool to admit this, but I did study. You're supposed to make being smart look effortless, but I studied hours every night for months with a book I got from the library. I even listened to this free SAT prep podcast I found, trying to make sure I could do my best. An SAT prep course is hundreds of dollars. I worked with what I could get for free. And it paid off. But it scared me how hard I had to work.

Wyatt looks around the table. "You guys toss these things off because you know you're smart. You don't have to be so . . . so . . . *disaffected* all the time."

"You're so sweet," Rei says. She kisses him on the cheek.

Trin snorts. "So what, you want her to hang her score above her bed or something?"

"That's where I keep my Boy Scout badges," Wyatt says.

"This I have to see," Rei says. Wyatt blushes. I'm a little surprised she's never been to his house. He's been to hers tons of times.

"Oh, I know," Trin says. "We should put it on a bumper

sticker! Like one of those white ones in an oval you always see. What are those for anyway?"

"Race distances," Wyatt says. "Like marathons and stuff."

"That's the ticket. Then your dad can put it on his truck."

Bumper stickers. Numbers. My brain refuses to think of it. 13.1, 26.2 . . . 1600.

I didn't apply to college, so it's not like I actually failed. You can't fail if you never try. But not trying is failing too, in its own way.

"How are you doing?" Lani asks me hesitantly.

"I'm going in the water for a minute," I say before I start crying.

~

I swim out as far as I can as fast as I can, past what's safe, farther than I've ever gone. In the evenings, this beach is crowded with surfers, and I should definitely not be out here. The waves try to slap some sense into me. I wish I could keep going forever.

Behind me, X is calling. I stop. I stare at the horizon and tread water. It's ridiculous to be looking for comfort in the distance when I know it's right behind me. I swim to shore, but it's the horizon I'm thinking about as I make my way out of the water, back to my friends. I have that annoying song from *Moana* playing in my head: . . . *there's just no telling how far I'll go.*

How far *will* I go?

140.6 miles?

Is that far enough to feel better?

And then, it's like when the chain on my bike winds itself into gear. Something has shifted, and my brain is grinding up a hill, finally making progress.

"I'm going to do an Ironman race," I say when I make it to the picnic table. The words just happen, my mouth calling the shots.

"The triathlon?" X asks.

"140.6 miles," I tell him. "Swim, bike, run."

My friends look at each other for a moment. Then they burst out laughing. All except Wyatt.

"So let me get this straight. You, who won't run a mile in PE even to pull yourself from a D to a C, who sat down in the middle of the floor during a basketball game because you didn't like running, are going to run 140.6 miles? In one go?" Trinity asks.

"No. I'm going to run 26.2 miles. After I swim 2.4 miles and bike 112 miles."

Trinity is laughing so hard she's crying.

"Why?" asks Rei.

"The universe pointed me to this race," I say. And it's more than that, I know. But it was a sign. Literally a banner.

"You feel like *she* pointed you to this race," X clarifies. "I saw her Instagram too, Miho. Basic."

"It's not . . ."

"Oh, it's not something you saw on her Instagram and immediately decided you needed to do to prove to your

Scumbucket ex-boyfriend that you're just as good as the girl he was two-timing?"

"No," I say, though . . . that sounds kind of accurate? Except it's more like, I need to prove it to the whole world, not just him. To all the Scumbuckets.

"Couldn't you just pull a *Wild* or something?" X asks.

"We're on an island, X. What am I going to do, walk in circles for four months?"

"You could climb Everest," Lani says, looking at her phone. "The internet says Ironman is a poor man's Everest."

"Yeah, well, I'm a poor man, and we're nowhere near Everest. But we are very near an Ironman race."

"It's like a thousand bucks even to get in," Trinity says.

I gasp, then I put it aside. I have to believe this is possible, even though I haven't seen a thousand dollars in my whole life.

"No, no, no," X says. "This is a dangerous and stupid idea, Miho. You can't do this."

"Yes I can. You said I was a fish of unusual size."

"Even fishes of unusual size have limits! You literally can't run a mile, Miho!"

"I mean, sorry, but I don't believe that," Wyatt cuts in. "Someone who can bike one hundred miles and then get up and deliver pizzas for six hours the next day can definitely run a mile."

Rei turns to him. "Wyatt, sweetie, you don't know Miho. She is all-caps Not A Runner."

"How do you know? Maybe it's my hidden talent," I say. "I mean, I've never failed because I've never tried."

“Okay, fine,” X says. “Run a mile in under ten minutes and we’ll say you can do it.”

He smirks at me. I hate him sometimes.

~

I am down, lunging like that’s some kind of magic power stance that will help me. The water laps up on the sand in front of me, making it solid enough to run on. On instinct, I take off my slippers, like that will make a difference.

I don’t listen as my friends count down from three. I don’t listen until the word “Go” strikes like a match on the lighter fluid flowing in my veins. The world swirls around me in strokes of blue and gold and I am off, unthinking, running as hard as I can.

To the tree and back. It’s only to the tree and back.

My brain whispers that I don’t know how to run, that I have no idea what I’m doing, that I look ridiculous. But I don’t have time for that. I clear my mind of all doubt as my feet hit the sand, my toes digging in, my arms pumping hard. I force my shoulders down, force air into my lungs, and think of nothing but the next step. It is my one and only thought.

I touch the tree, and it’s a half mile back.

I don’t think about how I’m slowing down.

I don’t think about my heart, and how it hurts.

I don’t think about her Instagram account full of moments she shared with the love of my life.

I don't think about how he probably doesn't even wonder about me, the way I wonder about his every moment.

I don't think about him forgetting me. I don't think about his wedding, and how he will look in his suit, and whether or not she'll carry his favorite flowers. I don't think about his swoopy hair, his eyes, his hands. His hands on me, him lying next to me, all the while lying *to* me.

And then I'm lit up by rage, barreling full power down the beach. My tears and sweat make the stars dance. They're alive the way Van Gogh saw them. I barely hear my friends yell. Everything is anger and pain.

But then I'm running past X, and I realize that was the finish line.

I did it. I don't feel anything at all.

~

"I can't believe it," Rei says. "Seven minutes *in the sand.*"

"Okay," I say, panting. I am still on my knees, unable to stand. "Now you guys have to say I can do it."

"I mean, we can *say* it. But that doesn't make it true," Trinity says. "I'm all for saying it. But have you thought about what it would take to *do* it?"

"We're talking about weeks where you train for eight-hour days. We're talking about a race that takes a lot of people almost seventeen hours to complete," Rei says. "I looked it up while you were running. It looks extremely hard."

"And do you honestly think that doing this will make you feel better?" X asks.

"I don't know. I think so," I say. "I'm picking a 'positive outlet' for my heartache. Isn't that exactly what you're supposed to do?"

"Not sure if a vengeance race fits the definition of 'positive outlet.'"

"It's not a vengeance race," I say. I scroll through a few pages on my phone. "Look. It says it right here on the Ironman website. 'Redefine possible.' That's what I want."

"It seems so . . . not you," X says.

"Who says what's 'me'?" I exclaim. "I want to do this. I want to try something different."

"You could do a million different things. Why *her* thing? Why are you jealous of her cruddy life? She's marrying a cheating pretentious bucket o' scum, and this all seems like a way of avoiding the fact that you're still in love with him. I mean, do you honestly want that beady-eyed little toadstool's Anthropologie wedding right out of the basic bitch catalog?" X asks.

"No," I say.

"So then why do you want her race?"

"Forget it," I say. It's like I've lost a race I never started.

"We could go egg her house instead," Trin offers.

"It's not about her."

". . . we could go egg *his* house?" Trinity tries.

"Seconded," Lani says.

"Thirded," Rei adds. They start to stand, presumably in pursuit of eggs.

"I think the race is a good idea," Wyatt says.

"What? Why?" I ask. Everyone sits back down.

"It sounds like a fun project," Wyatt says. "It's something we can all do together."

"We're not *all* doing an Ironman," Rei says.

"Count me way out," says Trinity.

"No, no, only Miho will do the race. But it could be a fun way for us all to . . . like . . . hang out and stuff," Wyatt says, growing more sheepish with every word.

"How will we do it together?" asks X.

Wyatt turns the piece of notepaper he's been scribbling on around. It's a bunch of lists. At the top, it reads, "Miho's Ironman."

"Well, it takes a lot of support to do a race like this. Miho needs a training plan, probably a nutritional plan, probably a new bike, there'll be lots of data from her workouts . . ."

"Oh, I totally call building the bike," Trinity says.

"I call nutrition, obviously, because Miho eats like a trash goat," Lani says.

"Well, Wyatt's got data, and I could build a training plan," Rei says. "If I taught myself to tap-dance for *Anything Goes,* I can definitely teach someone else to do a triathlon."

"What would I do?" asks X.

"You're the most important part. You're the coach," Wyatt says.

The air is humming. Something is about to happen.

"Oh, what the hell. I'm in," Trinity says at last. "This sounds like more fun than burning time until college. I could pass calc in my sleep."

"But are you sure you want to do this, Miho?" Wyatt asks. "You have to be completely sure. Absolutely sure."

"I am," I say. It's true.

"This is such a bad idea, but I'm excited," Lani says.

X squeezes my hand and leans over to whisper to me.

"I don't want you on the wrong side of 'What doesn't kill you makes you stronger,'" he says. "No shame if you want to stop. Just say the word."

I think about it. My heart is racing in anticipation. I don't know if I can do this, but I *can't* stop. I feel so light, like I'm flying. Maybe it will kill me, but right now, I feel stronger.

TRAINING

chapter eight

The next Saturday it's raining. Normally the rain passes quickly; the weather here changes every five minutes. But today it's raining like the island is conspiring with the sky to keep me off my bike.

Uncle Tua's is deserted. It's just me holding down the fort, and by holding down the fort, I mean watching paint dry. I have already done an accounting check on the till, wiped every surface, rolled all the silverware, even filled the little glass shakers with red pepper and fake parmesan. Now I'm getting paid eleven bucks an hour to sit here trying to balance a straw on my nose.

The boys are here too, of course, but the boys don't count toward fort-holding because they are idiots. In the best possible way, of course. When Tua isn't here, I'm in charge, even though they're all older than me. I get why. While I'm out here being responsible and not breaking the "no phones at the counter" rule even though I'd never get caught, they're in the back in their aprons and hairnets gathered around a phone, shooting a video for the latest Snapchat viral challenge. It's something involving a clapping game and lemons, and hopefully no one is getting hurt.

I give up on the straw and instead dig out all the chunks of fake cookie dough from four solid inches deep into the restaurant-sized tub of ice cream, exactly the way Uncle Tua has repeatedly told me not to. I knead the worthless vanilla back into a solid flatness for the tourists, then take my bounty out into the doorway, where I can still hear the phone in case I have to send one of the boys out in a car on delivery.

I'm bummed I can't be the one on deliveries today, but the rain is so beautiful and strange. I can't imagine how I used to live anywhere else. The colors here are magic, or maybe it's the light, because colors are made of light. Greens are more green. The sunsets demand the palette of a god. Even the lines are beautiful: the mountains are sound waves on the horizon, the trees are veins. This place is alive, speaking.

I wish I belonged here.

But I'm not Hawaiian.

I think about that every time I start to love this land or think I belong here. Even now, I feel like I'm a poser when I use Hawaiian slang or say I'm local. This could never be my home the way it's my friends' home, and I could never be Hawaiian the way Trin or Uncle Tua are Hawaiian. I only moved here in middle school after Dad had to take me in. But then, it's not like there's anywhere I *really* belong. Where would that be? California, where I was born? Which city? My mom and I moved so much, I was always on the outside. Plus, I'm mixed. I'm not Black like Lani, not Japanese like Rei, not even a drop Hawaiian, not whatever else is mixed up in there from my mom's side. I'm the one who doesn't belong, no matter where I am.

Well, that's not totally true. I look behind me into the restaurant. I look at all the tables ready for customers. I listen to the boys yelling; they must have gotten a good take.

I belong here.

I belong at Uncle Tua's. I belong to my tiny group of friends. I belong in the Trailer Park. But we all live in the real world too, and it's so complicated. Sometimes I wonder if we all belong to people and not to a place. If my tiny world got picked up and moved to Alaska, would we all feel at home? Or is part of what makes this home the ocean, the wind, and the rain?

The phone rings, and I thank the pizza gods for giving me an excuse not to think. Time for the afternoon rush.

Later, Tua comes in to help with the dinner crowd. Delivery starts to pick up, but Tua makes one of the boys do the deliveries because it's still raining so hard. I take care of a couple of families, regulars I know. I convince a couple of tourists to try my Heathen California Niece—named after me!—and suggest a few good hikes. A bunch of guys on my school's football team come in, and I help Tua shove a big table together for them. They don't recognize me, or even notice me, which is a relief. It's not that I'm embarrassed to work here. I wear my work shirt to school all the time, leave the pizza sign on my bike. It's more that when people think you have a connection, they try to get you to give them free stuff or alcohol, and I don't even do that for my friends.

In the best corner with the window, there's a big table of four couples who arrived in two matching Jeeps. They look like something out of one of the catalogs Rei always has spread all over her bed. Like somehow, wherever they go, massive bohemian tents and floor pillows and Moroccan-themed barware appear out of the mist, and they sit down to Instagrammable feasts, and then go on their merry way to the next forest or meadow or whatever is hip right now while the invisible ones clean up the mess they've left behind. I set out their plates and the pizza stand and notice their guidebook. Our restaurant was in *Lonely Planet* once, so we get a lot of these hip tourists from the mainland who want to feel local. I answer questions about the menu. The girls squeal at even the idea of Spam pizza. They ask Uncle Tua about secret bars, hidden gems, things "off the beaten path." Like we're stamps in the passport that proves they're really authentic.

"Look, this place makes historically accurate reconstructed rum cocktails from the eighteen hundreds." One of the guys points to something in his travel guide. He has stupid swoopy hair, tortoiseshell glasses, a J. Crew oxford unbuttoned to halfway down his chest.

"Is it organic?" asks his girlfriend.

He's talking about X's favorite restaurant, which we save up for and go to on his birthday. I keep my mouth shut. Why does it make me so mad that these mainland idiots are going there?

Why does it make me so furious that they like a place I like? Because they're getting it out of a book? Because if I were in their backyard, there's no way I could waltz into *their* favorite places, and yet somehow the world bends around these people here in my home?

In my fury, my tray tips and I drop a glass. It shatters, and all the boys in the back burst into applause. I laugh, take a bow, then take a breath. I look around and I'm here, in my favorite place where I belong, and these *Lonely Planet* wanderers will come and go forever and we'll laugh at them like we always do. We may be part of the scenery in their world, but they're also scenery in ours.

I think about that as I clean up the glass: it's like looking out a window. They're on one side of the window, I'm on the other. Like Van Gogh's window in his asylum. He painted a bunch of different views of the same wheat field he saw out that window, and so there are all these amazing paintings of the same place that he saw changing with the seasons. I think of working here like that. I see the same things, but they're different every time.

Except the thing is, Van Gogh's window wasn't exactly how he painted it. In reality, it had bars.

And sometimes, through my window, I don't see the wheat field. I see bars made of not enough money, of being the wrong color, of being worthless, of being someone you can throw away. I see bars made of *Will I ruin my life if I go to art school?* and *I look different than everyone else in this college application brochure* and *I don't know the rules here and everyone is staring.* And for a little while, with Scumbucket's hand in mine, I felt like maybe the bars were only things I'd imagined, and no one saw them but me. But now I think Scumbucket saw them, so he never took me seriously. We were holding hands, but I was on the other side of the bars.

Shoot. I hadn't thought about him for hours.

By the time I'm done cleaning up the glass, the couples are gone, and I can't even remember what I was so furious about. That's what I tell myself. But everywhere I look, I see the bars.

When I get off my shift, it's finally stopped raining. I catch a ride most of the way home on a delivery and walk the rest of the way. By the time I make it home, my friends are already hanging out in lawn chairs with sleeping bags set out all around on top of blue crinkly tarps. I'm the last to arrive, late for my own party. My neighbors are telling old war stories as Mr. Oshiro sets up the live stream. Mr. Oshiro's conspiracy-monitoring setup is also wonderful for stealing things off the internet and playing them on one of his projectors on a sheet in the yard.

"You girls need popcorn?" Mr. Kalani asks.

"Or drinks?" asks Mr. Bu.

"The audio is all wrong. Let me fix it for you," says Mr. Oshiro.

"Uncles, *please,*" I say, shooing them away as I drop my sleeping bag next to X. They retreat to my house, where Dad is barbecuing for all of us. They want to be included, I know, and I don't mind. But the race is about to start.

I look at the screen. Halfway across the world, there's about to be an Ironman. It's the first one I'll have ever watched.

I know abstractly what we're looking for: the women's pro race. But it's not like normal sports, where the people parade out to clips of terrible songs. I don't see anything but chaos. It's so many people you can't even figure out what's going on.

Then I get it. It's the fifteen-ish women right at the front, waiting to swim. They wear swim caps and wet suits. They're the ones competing for thousands of dollars. Maybe *a* thousand. Not sure.

"I can't watch twelve hours of people standing around," X says. "That's worse than baseball."

"You have not experienced hell until your dad makes you watch cricket," Lani says. "But this is getting close."

"We don't have to watch every second," I say. "I just want to see them start. We'll leave it playing and when we wake up, someone will have won."

"Too bad training by osmosis isn't a thing," Wyatt says.

"I still don't get it," Trinity pipes up. "When do they run? Where are all the bikes?"

Rei sighs very dramatically. She has been reading a book called *The Triathlete's Training Bible,* which is so massive that she had to switch her purse from her favorite Kate Spade crossbody to a Fjallraven Kanken backpack. She closes the book and stops the calculations she's doing on her phone.

"Okay, so it's #swimbikerun, right? So first you swim, then you hustle up after the swim, take the bike off the bar thing, and your shoes are *on* the bike—"

"It's all about the time," Wyatt bursts in. "When you change from swimming to biking, that's T1. Transition One. When you get off the bike and change for the run, that's T2. The time you spend changing shoes and clothes is on the clock. That's why they wear that one-piece outfit: so they don't have to change clothes between skills."

Trinity thinks hard. At last, she asks: "How do they, like, go?"

"I think it's called a rolling start, for swim safety, so no one dies," Rei says.

"Everyone who dies doing an Ironman dies on the swim leg," Wyatt confirms.

"Wait, *die*?" I ask. "Like, 'cease to exist' die?"

"Don't worry," he says. "Statistically, only middle-aged men die. You'll be fine."

Trin sighs, exasperated. "No, guys, I mean *go.* Like . . . you know. *Go.*"

We all look at her.

"Are you trying to ask how they pee?" I ask her.

We are silent.

Seventeen hours? You'd have to.

Rei is googling on her phone. "If you want to win, you pee in your wet suit and on the bike," she says. "Surprisingly common question."

"Ew," Lani says.

"Well, you're already wet from swimming and sweat," Wyatt says.

Lani grimaces. "That's so gross."

"You can use a porta-potty, but it slows you down," Rei says.

"Miho's in it to win it," Trinity says. "Sacrifices must be made."

"We don't have the money for the entry fee, so it's irrelevant," I say. "And how exactly do you pee in a space suit, Trin?" Everyone goes through an astronaut phase, but Trinity's not like other people. She's really going to be one.

"I'm thinking the moon is worth wetting yourself, and a triathlon is not."

"Maybe Ironman is my moon," I say. She thinks about that and turns back to the screen. I look too. The pros are swinging their arms, shaking out their legs, rolling their necks. I try to imagine myself there: my toes gripping the edge of the dock on the lake, the flying leap off, then the silence underwater for one moment until I break the surface again. I imagine the green-gray of lake water, nothing like the clear oceans here.

A gun sounds. Fifteen women dive and disappear into the lake. And I dive with them, in my mind.

It almost seems like something that could really happen. Almost.

~

My friends fall asleep in the yard before the first pro is even out of the water. I get it. It's late. I watch the camera pan over the lake, the age-group athletes churning the water white, the pros leading the pack. Over the past week I've watched every triathlon video I can find, from the triumphant finish-line clips, to training videos, to the famous moment when Julie Moss fell, then literally crawled her way to second place. I've gone back years through the social media of local tri clubs to see where they swim, what they wear, where they run.

I've never watched sports, but I can't turn away from the screen. These people half a planet away are doing this race *right now,* right this second, and watching it feels almost like doing it myself. The pro women are *so fast.* An hour to swim 2.4 miles. Five hours to bike 112 miles. A 3:30 marathon. That's 140.6 miles in under ten hours. Some of them can get under nine, though a lot depends on the course and the conditions. I stay up and follow along as complete strangers climb out of a lake and transform, one by one, into cyclists. In a few hours they'll all be runners.

Except, no matter how they change, none of them will be like me. You can tell just by looking at them, all hard edges and muscles in skintight Lycra. Maybe I could keep up the pace, but I'd wear the wrong shirt or something and then everyone would know. It's like when you go into a nice store, and you look around, and you realize you're the one dark face in a sea of white. No one points it out, but you clearly don't belong.

Everyone looks the same in a wet suit and swim cap, I remind myself. The fact that every person on that screen is skinny and white doesn't mean anything for me.

I head toward the house to pick over leftovers on the grill. Dad is awake, reading next to the warm coals.

"Hungry?" Dad asks. I nod, taking some chicken and sitting on the grass where I can still see the race. He squeaks over to me, then sits down with an "oomph" and kneads his half leg. I keep telling him to wear the nice prosthetic, but he's stupid stubborn. Dad lost his leg when he swerved his car into oncoming traffic back in California. He's lucky he's the only one who was hurt. I think he doesn't take care of himself because deep in his subconscious he thinks he deserved to lose his leg. Or maybe he's just lazy, and old, and a dad. Probably all of the above.

"They still swimming?" Dad asks.

"They're getting onto bikes now."

"Yes. Those bikes. Those very expensive bikes."

"I mean, mine will be fine with a few modifications," I say. He shakes his head, takes a piece of chicken right off my plate.

"Manners!" I say. He puts his pinkie out as he puts it in his mouth. I roll my eyes.

"Miho, I have looked into this race. I do not think you are considering the total cost."

"It's a little expensive," I say.

"Yes, it's over a thousand dollars to participate. A thousand, Miho, my flower. And that's just to get in. That doesn't cover where you would stay, or how you would get there, or even all the things you would need to do it."

"That's bananapants! Can I—"

"No."

"But you don't even know—"

"You're not getting a thousand dollars."

"But I need it."

"You don't need it. You want it."

"No, Dad, I *need* it. I need it like the wind needs the trees."

"Meaning?"

"I need to have something to ruffle. Otherwise I'm just air, Dad, raging against nothing. Without the trees, who would know the wind is blowing high above?"

"Anyone with the Weather Channel."

"Dad."

He rolls his eyes.

"I'll pay you back."

"No. Miho, you know better."

I bite my lip. Of course I know. And I know my dad is on disability, but that he works under the table doing odd jobs to make ends meet, and that he's already killing himself so that I can have things like a phone and birthday parties and even internet access. I've only been able to work since I was fourteen, and you can only work three hours a day until you're sixteen. But even though we're broke, Dad has never held food up as something I might not deserve, like my mom used to. I should be grateful.

Sometimes, though, I wish I could want things without feeling guilty.

But he's right. I do know better.

I do have some money I've been saving. I turn to Dad, who has clearly been watching the wheels in my head turning, but he shakes his head.

"You're not taking it out of your college savings either."

"DAD."

"I'm all behind your new interest in not mooning around and playing video games every day, but is it safe to do this thing?"

"Lots of people do it!"

"Also, you are not eighteen."

"But I will be."

"But you're not. And are you even sure you can finish?"

"My soul yearns to finish."

"Your soul is not the thing that has to power you across 140.6 miles."

"I can do this," I tell him. "The crew is going to help me train. All the Ironman signs say anything is possible."

"Yes, like getting into Harvard or West Point or even good old UH."

"Or, like swimming, biking, and running into a new era of Miho-hood. Miho 2.0, brought to you by the Ironman Corporation."

Dad sighs. I sigh louder.

"If I had a thousand dollars, I'd buy you a little perspective and some common sense to go with it. You don't even have a bike. Do you know how much a bike like that costs?"

"I can do it on my bike."

"Your bike has a basket on it, Miho. And a pizza rack—"

"Well, it's not welded to the frame!"

"—and the cut-off ends of ribbons on the handlebars. Maybe I can get you some shoes, if you want some real running shoes. You could run the Honolulu marathon in December! The entry for that is pretty expensive, but I looked into it, and your uncles and I might be able to get it together."

"But it has to be an Ironman," I say, tears prickling in my eyes. "Dad, it has to be."

"Miho. Listen. I think it's great that you want to do this. But look up the bike. Look it up."

"Holy mother," I shout as the search results for "Triathlon Bike" light up my phone. Achilles sits up at the sound, lets out one startled yip, but then flops onto his back and falls asleep with his tongue hanging out. "How can a bike cost twelve thousand dollars?" I whisper.

"Exactly, Miho. Pick something a little more reasonable."

"I'm sick of reasonable. History is not full of reasonable women."

"I don't know why you want to set yourself up to fail."

"Isn't that exactly what you're trying to do, with this whole college thing?"

"It's not the same."

"Something that seems impossible, costs a ton of money, and inspires some dedicated people to work insanely hard and beat the odds? It's exactly the same."

He narrows his eyes at me. I narrow mine right back.

He breaks first, sighs, throws up his hands.

Point: Miho.

chapter nine

I watch all night. When the crew wakes up, I try to make the play-by-play of the race sound exciting, but even I can't turn it into a spectator sport: "And then, on the run, the one lady passed the other lady, and then she got passed again forty minutes later!" The most exciting things in triathlon are (1) flying dismounts gone awry and (2) that time Heather Jackson carried a banana during the entire marathon in somewhere called Lake Placid. The only other exciting thing that happens are crashes, and those are scary, not funny.

Normal people have "running but not getting anywhere" or "in class naked" dreams. I have bike crash dreams. They always start out happy: I'm riding down the coast on a completely empty highway, the wind at my back. I'm flying. But then out of the blue, with no warning, I crash. I hit a rock, or a car hits me, or my bike falls apart underneath me into a pile of wheels and gears. I hit the ground, and it *hurts*. But that's not the worst part. After I fall, I can't move. My dream-body is bleeding and broken, and I am forced to stare at where I crashed. I always think: I should have seen it coming. I should have been more careful. Because it's obvious *after* you crash: you shouldn't have been on that road, you should have seen the pothole, you should have seen the car. And I lie there for an eternity in dream-time, and no one can help me.

If I ever have a crash like that, in real life, I honestly don't know if I'll ever ride again.

Dad left before dawn to see if there are any jobs, so Mr. Bu calls us over to his house for coffee and breakfast. We sit on his porch with our legs dangling off the edge, plates of sausage, eggs, and rice in our laps. Then everyone goes home to change. I rush through my chores—dog, trash, weeds, pay bills, prep dinner, do laundry—and head to my room. I put on some old sweatpants, dig out my one and only sports bra, throw on a work shirt with the sleeves cut off, and try to find my old gym shoes from PE. At last, I excavate them from my completely overflowing closet, under a pink linen button-up shirt.

My heart jumps. I pull my hand back. Scumbucket's shirt.

It's like poison from a snakebite crawling up my arm. The sleeves are still rolled up *just so,* exactly the way he left it. I know I should throw it away, but . . . I don't. I will when I get home. Definitely.

I look at my phone. Twenty minutes to get to the track. I pull on my shoes and close the closet door.

At the track, I don't even make it three feet before Rei is shaking her head, marching over from the others. I want to go over and see what's in Lani's picnic basket, but Rei is standing in front of me with her hands on her hips.

"No good?" I ask.

"First of all, what is this thing you are wearing? You are going to chafe like hell."

"They're called sweatpants."

"Second of all, what is on your feet?"

I look down. My sneakers are old and a little battered, but they're not falling apart or anything.

"Show me the soles," Rei prompts.

I lift my leg up to show her and she grabs me by the ankle, sending me falling backward into the grass.

"See this big flat spot on the bottom?" she asks. I take my foot back, twisting my leg so I can see.

"Yeah?" I ask. From the look on her face, I can tell that I should totally know why these shoes shouldn't have flat spots on the bottom. When it becomes clear that I don't have an answer, she throws up her hands.

"You're a size seven?" she asks. I nod. "My sister is too. Let me see if she has any hand-me-downs that aren't cleats."

"I can buy new shoes." My cheeks are burning.

"Oh, please, she tosses hers out brand-new if she doesn't like the laces," Rei says.

Trinity is waving wildly at us, saving me from declining the sneakers. The truth is, shoes are expensive AF, and it won't be the first time I've taken clothes secondhand from Rei and her sisters. Rei doesn't even remember: these shoes were her sister's too.

Over by the picnic basket, there's a big lab notebook spread out on the grass. Wyatt is busily copying something out of one of Rei's gold-speckled notebooks.

Wyatt flips the notebook so I can see it. He's turned it into a dated diary, like a planner on Instagram. It's got spaces for what I ate, my planned workouts, my actual workouts, even what shoes I wore. Pages and pages.

Today we're doing a run workout. It's called a "benchmark" session. Then tomorrow I do a bike benchmark, and then the next day a swim benchmark. Rei says that, according to her book, we shouldn't be doing these so close to each other, but since we're short on time, we'll work with what we've got.

"Short on time?" I ask.

"People train for these things for a year minimum," Rei says. "We've got six months."

"So I'll train twice as hard," I say.

"You can't," Wyatt says. "You can only ramp up your training so fast before you're doing more harm than good."

"Then I'll want it twice as much," I say, tightening the laces on my shoes.

"For anyone else, I'd say this is impossible," Rei says. "But you already bike well over ten hours a week."

"How's that?"

"Thirty minutes to school and thirty minutes back gets you to five. Then there's pizza deliveries. Let's say you're on your bike sprinting like hell an hour out of every four-hour shift—"

"Way more than that!"

"But for the sake of argument. You work, what, five shifts a week? So we're at ten. And that's conservative."

"So, piece of cake," I say.

"We'll see," Rei says.

The run benchmark is simple. First I jog around the track for ten minutes, which isn't too bad. Then when Rei hits the button on her timer and yells "Go!" I'm supposed to run as hard as I can for twenty minutes. I start off strong, sprinting like I did on the beach. But by the time I do the first lap, I'm ready to lie down and die. I'm back to a jog. The others cheer me on. I start walking. Cheers turn to taunts.

I want to keep running, but I can't catch my breath. I keep walking, trying to force my legs to jog. In my head I make deals with myself: When you get to that line, start jogging. When the old guy power walking passes you, start jogging. Come on, legs! Just freaking do it!

But I can't.

X jogs over. I realize the group has gotten quiet, but I'm too embarrassed to look.

"Is that the best you can do?" X walks beside me.

"No," I groan, and start jogging again. He runs next to me, even though he's wearing his favorite brogues.

"A little faster," he says, looking at his watch. "Slow down," he says when I start sprinting. We do one full lap, matching steps, and then he peels off. This time, I hold the pace. I'm running slower than the old people out here jogging, and it's taking all of my willpower to keep going. "I think I can, I think I can,"

I chant in my head, one word per step. It feels ridiculous, but it keeps me on pace. It is the longest twenty minutes of my life. When Rei calls time, I sit down on the track.

Rei trots over. "Okay, so that went . . . less well than I had hoped," she says, standing over me.

"How far did I make it?"

"Including the warm-up? Three miles."

"Are you kidding me? That was only three miles?"

I'm a little ashamed of myself. I tried so hard.

"A ten-minute mile is totally respectable," X says. I put my head in my hands. I thought I'd be knocking out seven-minute miles no problem, like I did that first day. X, reading my mind, continues: "I mean, training is not a race, and your mile time is different from your 5K time, which is different from your 10K time . . ."

"I know. I just wanted to be good at this," I say.

"Then don't give up before you even start," X says.

"Don't worry, Mi-kins. *It's not where you start, it's where you finish,*" Rei sings.

If you finish, I think.

~

X drops me off at home. My legs ache. My feet burn. My whole back hurts.

I wander into the house, past the complaints of my dog and the yapping of my dad and neighbors. In my room I fall face-first onto my pillow and take a nap, my sweat-soaked hair making the pillow unpleasantly damp.

I wake up two hours later. I stretch out and, much to my surprise, I don't feel that bad. A little sore, but not horrible. I stand up. I can walk. I take a shower. I go out to the living room.

"Lazy Sunday?" Dad asks. I shrug. The neighbors are gone. Achilles brings me a yellow tennis ball, and I open the front door and pitch it away as far as I can. You think of throwing as something you do with your arms, but it turns out it's not. Everything is connected. The ball lands pathetically close in the yard, and I can feel up and down my sides exactly which muscles are used in running, because they're the ones saying "hard nope."

Aki passes me by on attempt two of fetch. Harsh. Dad takes the ball and, without even getting off the love seat, pitches it out the open door. Achilles gallops after it, bites it on the steps, somersaults onto the grass, then continues running like nothing even happened.

"I thought you were training for an Ironman," Dad says.

"I ran like a million miles this morning."

"A million?"

"Well, three."

Dad laughs, returns to the paper.

"Well, how far did you run today?" I snap, sinking into the love seat.

He raises an eyebrow at me and nods toward his prosthetic leg. I roll my eyes.

"You can run with the other hook-looking one," I say. "You're just lazy."

"Disabled."

"Yeah, right. You're selectively disabled. You're not disabled when you hear there's a sale on at Costco. I've seen you sprint down those aisles."

He laughs. "Old, at least. You can give me old."

"Yeah, that's true. But lots of old people run. Or at least power walk."

"If I power walked, people would go blind from a mere glimpse of it."

"There's a famous triathlete named Sister Madonna who still does Ironman triathlons. She's older than you."

"How are there famous triathletes?"

"I mean, they're not *famous* famous. They're famous to people who do triathlons. Kind of like how Tua is famous in one town only."

"So they're the local celebrities of triathlon-ville."

"More like triathlon-polis. Triathlopolis? Whatever. Triathlon is super popular, Dad. It's huge. And there are tons of Paralympic triathletes. All those blind people who had the misfortune to see you power walking can do the race with a guide."

I bite my lip. I know better than to push this. "You could do a triathlon if you wanted," I say.

"140.6 miles? No, Miho. I could not."

"But there are shorter ones. Like you could do a sprint or something. Maybe it would be fun. Or just . . . swim, *or* bike, *or* run. You know, kind of like they tell you to at the clinic? Like literally every time you go?"

"You know, I did used to jog," he says, putting down his newspaper.

"You should take it up again," I say, stretching out my legs. Ouch. "Or not. Running sucks."

Dad runs his hands over his belly, a remnant of when he drank beer.

"Maybe," he says. "Maybe I should."

I spend the rest of the afternoon hanging out on the love seat with him. He reads and I grab a sketchbook. I haven't drawn or painted anything in a while. I didn't feel like it after . . . everything. Normally, I paint and draw almost as much as I bike. How many hours a week? Ten? At a minimum.

It's a different kind of energy than biking, but when I'm painting, time vanishes like it does when I'm riding. I disintegrate into this weird focus where the world falls away but I also notice everything. It's like the me that is nervous, or sad, or angry, or happy, or in love, isn't even there. I'm a gear being turned by forces outside myself. Mr. Bu told me that's the peace you're supposed to get from meditation. But I hate meditation. I'd rather bike and paint.

I want to sketch my dad the way I see him, but I put my pencil to the pad and it doesn't move. It's like it doesn't know which way to go, because it doesn't know what I *really* see. So I think about how I would put my dad on paper. How would I put into lines the way it makes me sad, all the things he doesn't do because he thinks he's disabled? Why can't he be like Aki and run after the metaphorical ball?

And how would I sketch out how I love him now, but I also know that he abandoned me before I was even old enough to talk? That "dad" didn't even make it into my first five words? How could I possibly paint the way that I know, abstractly, that he used to be a very bad person, but I can't see it because I never met that person?

The picture in my mind is so complicated that I can't imagine making it two-dimensional. This is why it's easier to copy Van Gogh.

I look at my paper. It's blank.

That's what happens when I think too hard about drawing.

I'm worried I'm going to think myself out of this race. Because, the second I stop to think about it, I realize how far 140.6 miles actually is, how I don't have the money to pay for the entry, how I've never even played a sport—

Stop. One step at a time.

I look at my sketch pad again. One step. One line. I force myself not to think, and I draw a quick sketch of Dad, loose and easy. And it's not perfect. It doesn't say *everything* I want to say. But it's there, on the page. And there's something in it that I like. A tiny thing: the way the paper he's reading looks like it's fluttering in his hand. But that one tiny thing is better than the nothing I had before.

I go to my room. I put my sketchbook into my art box and start rearranging the stuff that's all out of order from when I threw it across the room. I still feel like I'll never paint again without thinking of Scumbucket. But that's only a feeling. Rationally, I know it isn't true.

I look at the closet, go to throw that shirt away.

As I put my hand on the closet door, I hear the front doorbell, which Dad had Mr. Oshiro turn into a crow's caw with some stupid thing they ordered on the internet, so every time someone rings it, it sounds like there's a crow in the house. It was supposed to be "for me," but it was obviously something he wanted, like the Lego set in the living room we used to play with all the time, which mysteriously builds itself into fortresses while I'm at school. Dad wanted to be an architect. He was a construction worker; now he's a day laborer.

"Your boyfriend's here!" Dad calls back into my room. My heart leaps for one instant, but in almost the same moment, I realize who he's talking about. I actually have to steady myself on a chair, my chest hurts so bad. Why does heartbreak have to feel like heartbreak? Maybe it's all connected, like running isn't only in your legs, and throwing isn't only in your arms.

I grab my bag, and when I set foot in the living room, it's X I'm expecting, and it's X I'm glad to see. Tonight we're binge-watching TV at his house: our current obsession, this old show from the '60s, *The Avengers.* It is . . . of varying quality.

"Let's go, boyfriend."

chapter ten

A few nights later, my friends come by to meet me at the end of my shift, which is when things are starting to pick up. The late lunchers have given way to the dinner rush, and every table is full. Now all I see around me are orders and table numbers. I get so caught up in it that it's hard for me to head out, even though my shift is over.

I throw off my apron when I see Trinity tapping her watchless wrist in the doorway. I worked fifteen minutes over already.

"Sorry," I tell Tua. "You want me to stay?"

"You're done. Get out," he says. "Go do teenager things. But good teenager things."

Uncle Tua hands me a fat stack of bills—my tips, which I of course report to the IRS the way I'm supposed to—and off I go feeling a little rich, the way a good tip night always makes you feel.

"Gangsta," says Trinity, looking at the money. I flip through it.

"Singles," I explain. It's probably eighty bucks, though. Very good night. I will say mainlanders tip extravagantly. If I could only have a few weeks of nights like this, and didn't spend a dollar of what I earned, that would be the entry fee. Except, of my tip money and paychecks, most will go to my "college savings" fund, siphoned off by Dad into an account I promised him I would not touch. A promise is a promise. Dad takes care of food, but I buy my own clothes, and I need new everyday shoes because my feet hurt. My Van Gogh sneakers were comfy. My old Converse are not much better than socks at this point. I put it off too long because I also need a rain jacket, but now I think the shoes are more important. I also buy some things Dad doesn't understand, like tampons and birth control. It adds up.

So it might take a few months of good tip nights. Except I don't have a few months. Maybe if I make do with my old shoes—

"I don't care what Lani tells you, you save your pennies for bike parts," Trinity says. "Bike trumps food."

"It's irrelevant, because I don't have the entry fee," I say.

Trinity is grinning like she has something up her sleeve, and I refuse to get my hopes up, but they're already up. I can't help myself. Maybe there *is* a miracle out there. God knows I need one.

Everyone is sitting between the open doors of Rei's Prius and X's ancient beat-up Honda, making our own little clubhouse out in the parking lot.

They get up as we approach. Trinity backs away from me, raising her hands to make an announcement.

"So, you're *not* doing an Ironman," Trinity says. "There is no way we can raise that much money."

"Yeah, thanks, I got that," I say. Trinity holds up a finger.

"Instead, you're doing a Miho . . . man!" Trinity shouts. Lani unfurls a sloppily painted poster she's been hiding behind her back, and Rei throws some jazz hands in front of it. "A Miho-man?" Trinity tries it out again, looking around with a quizzical bend to her eyebrows. Rei shakes her head.

"I told you it wouldn't sound cool," Rei says. The poster, which has "First Annual Miho-man" painted in kiddie tempera, features a somehow out-of-proportion stick figure swimming, biking, and running.

"I kind of like it," Wyatt says.

"It sounds like a Japanese superhero. Like One-Punch Man," Lani says.

"Well, Iron Man is a superhero. So it works," Trinity says.

"Can't we call it something that doesn't end in 'man'? For feminism?" Rei asks.

"Doesn't 'woman' end in 'man'?" Wyatt asks.

"Wow. Just . . . wow." Rei swats him playfully.

"Guys, what the hell are you talking about?" I break in.

Trinity shushes everyone. "We'll work on the name. And the logo. We need something that'll look cool on a T-shirt. But the point is, you don't have to do a stupid expensive Ironman race. You can do the same race without the branding and we can work it basically for free."

"How exactly?" I ask.

"We can't get you into an Ironman race, but you can do

what's called an Iron-*length* race. 140.6 miles, but without the corporate bullshit," Trinity says.

"Okay," I say, a little confused.

"Wyatt and I spent the day at the computer lab at the community college looking at topographical maps. We think it's the best choice," Trinity says.

"And the only choice," Wyatt admits.

"But therefore the best choice. And besides, this way, we can choose the date ourselves."

"It'll be exactly like the *original* Ironman," Wyatt says. "Like, vintage."

"The bad news is: apparently, you aren't technically an Ironman unless you do one of their 'M-Dot' races, even if it's exactly the same distance," Rei says.

"So I won't be an Ironman. I'll be a . . . Miho-man," I say, trying to keep the disappointment out of my voice.

"Which is *better* than an Ironman," Lani says. She shakes the sign cheerily.

"Look at it this way: some people be like, 'Oh that Gucci, that's hella tight!' " Rei says. "But we're like, 'That's just some ignorant bitch shit.' "

No one says a word about Rei's Kate Spade bag, dangling from the crook of her arm. But I see X glance at it, and I see her follow his eyes. The moment passes, almost like it never happened.

"What do you think?" X asks. I smile, and try to make it look like a real one.

"It's perfect," I say, because it's the best we can do. Trinity pulls out her phone and shows me a map. It's pretty close to where we live. I've biked most of the places she's showing me. Just not all at once.

"That's a lot of road," I say. My brain translates maps into minutes pretty quickly from delivery work. A lot of road is an understatement. I hadn't let myself think about what that distance would look like on the land I know so well. The whole island is only 114-ish miles around the circumference. They've got the path wiggling around what they think are roads without a lot of cars, but that will mean taking turns at high speed, or slowing down. I'll have to practice.

"What's the cutoff time again?" I ask.

"For the swim, it's a maximum time of two hours, twenty minutes. The bike cutoff is eight hours, ten minutes, no problem for you there, and the run cutoff is six hours, thirty minutes," Wyatt says.

"Seventeen hours total," X says.

"We have the whole rule book," Trinity says. "We're going to make sure it's exactly, to the letter, to the decimal, to the quark, the exact same race. So no one can ever say you're not just as good as an Ironman."

Just as good as, I think. But I won't *be* an Ironman.

"Seventeen hours. Christ," I say.

"You'll beat seventeen. We're already taking bets on this, and mine was thirteen and a half hours," X says. "It's a twenty-dollar buy-in if you want to play."

"That seems unethical. What did you bet?" I ask Wyatt.

"I don't make bets of faith. Once I have an estimate of your

VO2 max and lactate threshold, I'll use your training plan and, anticipating deviations, calculate—"

"You can't tell her what time she's going to get, Wyatt," Rei says. "It'll ruin the race."

"I could be wrong."

"You won't be. We'll put all our bets in a secret envelope and open them after the race."

"Seems fair," I say.

"Well, I don't care who knows. I bet nine hours flat," Trinity says.

"That's ridiculous," Lani says. "That's faster than the pro times. We don't want to set unreasonable expectations."

"This whole race is an unreasonable expectation."

"Fair," I throw in. "But nine hours isn't happening."

"I am so psyched!" Trinity grabs me by the shoulders. "I am going to build the hell out of your bike!"

"Before we trick out our toys, though, we have to tackle the boring stuff," Rei says.

"Like what?" asks Trinity.

"The actual training part," says Rei. "And looking at your benchmarks . . . we've got a long way to go."

I sigh.

"Can't we upload all of that into my brain *Matrix*-style?"

"Training montage!" Trinity shouts. She pauses dramatically mid-run, as though she expects the scene to cut.

Lani shakes her head. "This is going to be a long six months."

chapter eleven

A finger pokes me in the ribs. I keep my eyes closed.

It pokes me again and this time I grab it.

"Trinity," I growl.

"Ow, beast! Teacher's looking at you," Trinity says under her breath, cradling her hand. "Get your head up."

I manage to pull my face off my drool-coated worktable and set it on my hands so that I can maintain at least a simulacrum of wakefulness.

Simulacrum. A Scumbucket pain shoots through me. Little memories hurt the worst, when they creep up on you like that.

Simulacrum means "a fake version of something." When Scumbucket was reading this book called *Simulacra and Simulacrum*, he explained to me that it's way more complicated than that and we're all living in the Matrix, but basically, that's what it means. So: I am a simulacrum of myself today. Even my fingers are tired. Even my blisters have blisters. Yesterday's training sessions about broke me. That's *sessions. Plural.* I have never been this sore in my whole life.

Our teacher, Mrs. Miller, is not fooled. It's February and she's already got each of us pegged: potheads, troublemakers, dumb but earnest, smart but lazy. I see her eyeing me as she talks and talks about Picasso's blue period and the color wheel.

"And what is it called when we use *only one* color?" she asks.

"Monochromatic," the class repeats in monotone. I mumble along, trying to shake her eyes off me.

I should be in AP Art History, not stupid remedial art, but I didn't have the prerequisites. I bet in AP Art History you get to talk beyond the fact that the paintings are—wait for it!—*blue,* and into who he was portraying, and why. When Mrs. Miller tells us the paintings are blue because Picasso was sad, my eyes about roll into the back of my head. Yeah, lady. That's everything that was going on. Blue equals sad.

She's going to talk for the next ten minutes exactly because that's what it says on our lesson plan. She's evil-eyeing the potheads in the corner now as she lists colors and the feelings they magically map onto for literally every human ("Red equals angry!" Well, not if you're Chinese, Teach), so I slide my phone out.

Nothing. Not even a message from X.

I get it. We're all in school.

I used to check for messages from Scumbucket a hundred times a day, and I haven't quite broken the habit. We texted constantly: in school, late at night, even sometimes when I was at work, I'd sneak into the back room and catch up. It was like he was always right next to me, even though he wasn't there. My entire life and heart was in this phone.

Now that I think about it, how real was it? We only saw each other once a week, sometimes not even that. We only really hung out online. Going to Amsterdam, being together forever . . . those were only promises.

I look around. Half my class is on their phones, the screens hidden in their laps and beneath their desks. Even Trin next to me is compulsively reloading her in-box, waiting to hear from MIT. Everyone is on their phone constantly now. I'm sure no one would notice him sending off hundreds and hundreds of messages and pictures. He never sent me any of "Byron," but sexting is so easy. Everyone here could have a secret side chick, and no one would know.

But does that make it "not real"? Was I like an app to him? Something he could delete when he was bored of me? A simulacrum of a girlfriend.

I look at my phone. My fingers hover over the screen.

It's not that I'm checking. Not that I have this constant voice inside me saying, *Maybe you missed his reply!* Not like I'm lying to myself, heading into Themria looking for him every night, even though I can see he hasn't been on since we broke up.

I open our text messages.

Still nothing.

"Give it here," Mrs. Miller says, and an open palm passes under my eyes.

"What?" I ask. She picks the phone up off my lap, puts it in her apron.

"No phones in class. Now tell me, Miho, since you've been paying such keen attention: What does it mean when a painting is *yellow*?"

She says the word *yellow* super clear, like I might misunderstand this complicated term. She stands over me, smirking. My mouth won't form words; it hangs open in disbelief. I hear the potheads guffawing in the corner. Mrs. Miller grins, like she knows she's got me, like I'm too stupid to know the answer to this obviously stupid question.

"Class, what does it mean—"

"It depends who you're asking. I think," I get out before she can finish. She turns to look at me like she's astonished I have the capacity for speech, and I rush on before she can stop me. "I mean, like, the question doesn't make sense. Sometimes it means, 'Hey wow like yellow paint is easy to make so I'm gonna use it all over this cave wall' and sometimes it means, 'I gotta have something to set off all this blue,' like for Picasso, and yeah, sometimes it means, you know, 'This painting is optimistic.' But, like, if you think about it, lots of Van Gogh's paintings are full on yellow, and I don't think it means he was happy or that the painting is like happy. Like colors don't work that way. I think."

Stupid. Stupid Stupid Stupid. California *like*. Oh my god I sound like an *idiot*. Why can't I talk like the smart person I am?

Teacher pauses, looking me over. I should have let her shame me. It's more words than I've said this whole semester, because usually we spend class repeating what she says so we learn the "vocabulary." There's no discussion. Number one lesson I have learned in every new school: you are invisible, or you are embarrassed.

"That's a good point," Mrs. Miller says. Everyone goes back to repeating colors and emotions.

But she doesn't give me back my phone.

~

We finally settle into the "art" part of class: making a color wheel out of a drawing of something we like. Mine's a pizza with the toppings done in complementary colors. Trin's is a bunch of rockets taking off, which is cool. I finished mine two days ago, so I put it out in front of me like it's waiting on finishing touches and pull my own sketchbook out of my backpack and into my lap. I quickly sketch Trin working so hard to paint in the rockets.

"It's a good likeness," a voice says behind me, and before she can take it, I shove my sketchbook under my T-shirt, straight-up ripping a hole in the front. Mrs. Miller laughs.

"This is art class. You're welcome to work on your own art projects once your classwork is finished," she says. "Where have you been hiding all this talent and insight, Miho?"

"I haven't been hiding it," I say sheepishly. "It's just that no one ever notices."

"I notice," Trinity says defensively. She looks at Mrs. Miller and holds up her rockets hopefully. "A?"

"Dripping," Mrs. Miller points out. Trinity swears like a sailor and tries to right her watercolors.

"See me after class for your phone, Miho," Mrs. Miller says. "Next time it's going to the principal's office, but I think we can let it slide just this once. And Trinity, put that away right—"

"It's here," Trin says breathlessly.

She turns around her phone, tears brimming in her eyes.

"The email," she says. "I'm going. I'm really going."

"Where?" Mrs. Miller asks.

"MIT," Trinity says. She looks down at her dripping rockets. "I'm going," she says. I want to hug her, but she's not a hugging person. And she doesn't seem like she's happy. Her hands are shaking and she's barely breathing. "I'm going," she says again. Then she picks up her stuff and leaves, straight-up cutting class in front of a teacher.

"She, uh . . . has to go collect herself," I tell Mrs. Miller.

"I didn't see anything," Mrs. Miller says, putting a finger to her lips. "As far as I know, she was here until the end of the day."

"That's cool of you," I say.

"Of course. After all, it's a very special occasion."

~

After class, I waddle my sore butt up to Mrs. Miller's desk and hold out my hand. My other hand is holding the hole right in the front of my T-shirt closed so my bra isn't showing. If I flip it around so it's backward, I can change into one of the logo shirts that got messed up at the screen printers so they say

Uncle Tuba's Pizzeria, which Tua keeps in a box in the break room because they're hilarious. It's my last class, and I've only got an hour to stop at the grocery store and get to Tua's, which isn't normally a problem, but my legs are totally dead from yesterday. Even walking hurts.

"You kids just can't live without these things," Mrs. Miller says, my phone on her desk. Given that she's, like, forty at a stretch, I'm pretty sure she has a phone, and this is just something she thinks she has to say because she's an adult. She looks at me over her glasses intensely, and it's kind of weird. I withdraw my hand. I don't know what she wants.

"Yeah, sorry," I say. "Won't happen again."

"Miho, I was impressed by what you said in class today. I wish you would speak up more."

"It seems kind of . . . pointless," I say. "I mean, no one in class cares about art."

"I care. And you seem to care."

I nod. "I'll try to say things in class," I say, glancing at the clock. I can get to my locker and out the door in ten minutes, and if I stop for groceries on the way to work and put them in the work fridge, then I can trade laundry duty with Dad and get in that last sprint session after work if I do my homework on my break—

"Listen, Miho. I'm trying to help you. Kids like you, it's not that you're not smart, it's that you're lazy," she says.

I stop my mental calculations.

"Huh?"

"You are a talented artist and a smart girl, Miho." She smiles.

"It's just a cultural thing. That's not your fault, it's just a fact. So you'll have to work a little harder to overcome that and learn how successful people behave. Successful people don't phone in their assignments. They don't give the minimum effort. They give it their all. Like Trinity. Think of everything she's overcome."

"Okay," I say, my face getting red.

"I want you to succeed, but you need to show me that you want that too. You can be better than this." She finally hands me back my phone. "I'm here for you."

"Thanks." I shove it in my pocket.

I speed-walk to my locker, as fast as my sore legs will carry me. I open the door, grab my stuff, slam it hard.

Teachers are all like that. Think I'm lazy. Think I don't try. Do they have any idea how I live? No. Well, sorry I didn't "give my all" to your stupid color wheel for kindergartners. Maybe I was busy giving my all to the job that lets me have clothes to wear, and the chores I do to keep my house running, and all the other ways I have to work harder than people who get to be in AP Art History classes.

You know what I'm going to work hard at? The things I actually care about. Like *my* art. Screw her color wheel. And you know what else? I'm going to work hard at swimming, and biking, and running. I am making the time to work hard on that, on top of *everything else* I work hard at. Because if you work hard, at the end of all that work you can race 140.6 miles in a single day, and no one can ever doubt that you know how to put in the work ever again.

chapter twelve

I'm up early on Saturday. I'm meeting Rei in the afternoon, and I need to get in my bike-run brick, which is a five-hour workout. I also need to get the groceries, do all my chores, and work on my midterm problem set for calculus.

I swear under my breath as I leave the house when I see the chair. Today, of all days?

Haircutting day is once a month. Mr. Kalani wakes up, gazes at the sky with a sailor's intuition, and feels in his bones that the day has come. He makes the coffee and, with an instinct equal to the compulsion felt by migratory birds, drags the haircutting chair out onto the lawn. He finds the navy surplus bag he uses to store his nice scissors in his massive cabinet of art supplies and ceremonially sets out his tools. Then, he drinks his coffee and waits, meditating on the transitory nature of existence and the eternal battle of man against growth that haircutting represents.

That last part I'm not sure about. He's probably thinking about football games that happened ten years before I was born.

"Miho, I'm ready," Mr. Kalani says, gesturing to the chair. I sling my stuff up onto the porch and sit down.

"Any requests?" he asks.

"Don't mix me up with my dad and give me a buzz cut," I say. Our running joke. He laughs, like he always laughs, then dumps water over my head so that my hair won't be too crooked.

Scissors snip. I glance at the time on my phone. Maybe if I don't say anything, this will go quickly.

Mr. Kalani's haircuts aren't bad. They're neat and military grade. Still, I've always kind of wondered if maybe getting my hair cut by a real professional would make me look pretty, if maybe that's the difference between me and those girls with shiny, flowing locks. But Mr. Kalani's haircuts are free, and when I looked at the price of a "real" haircut, I vomited a little bit. Even if I could pay for it once, I couldn't afford to keep going back over and over. So I just have to live with feeling ugly.

I know I'm supposed to say I love my "curly" hair. But I don't. My hair is what the internet calls "3C curls." My dad has a buzz cut and is a man; he has no idea what I'm supposed to do with it. When I was a kid, my mom let it go, put it in two little frizzy balls when I went to school, and told me to focus on math instead of on my appearance.

No matter what I do, my hair is a frizzy mess. I have followed so many YouTube videos, and nothing makes a difference. I hate having curly hair more than anything else about myself. I would be okay with being chubby, with having a funny nose, with my weird eyes, with my thunder thighs, if I could just have shiny hair like Rei does, like every girl I see in a magazine.

I am who I am, and there's nothing I can do about it. And all of this is a part of who I am: the haircuts at home, the curly hair, the girl attached to it. And what sucks is that I love getting my hair cut by Mr. Kalani. I wish I were beautiful, but I can't have it both ways. I can't be me and be beautiful. It's nobody's fault. It's just the way it is.

I wipe my tears. I'm seventeen. Crying over my hair? This is pathetic. The scissors pause.

"What's wrong, Miho?"

"Nothing," I say, laughing.

"Miho."

"Really. Nothing," I say.

The scissors start again. But I can't listen to my brain anymore.

"Do you ever wish you were someone else?" I ask after a few minutes. He thinks for a moment.

"The Duke," he says. "My first girlfriend had a big crush on him."

"The Duke?"

"Duke Kahanamoku! The father of surfing. Anyway, he died when she was a little kid, so you think: no real competition. But you ever try competing with an idea? Can't win; an idea does no wrong. Who do you wish you were? Van Gogh?"

"I don't think it was very fun to be Van Gogh," I say. "I don't wish I *was* him, I wish I understood him."

"Who, then? Your old movie lady? Myrna Loy?"

"Yeah," I say. "That'd be nice. To be pretty like Myrna Loy."

"Pretty? I thought you meant rich. And talented. And charming. But you already are those things. Except rich."

But I can't answer him. If I open my mouth, I'm going to start crying again.

After a minute, he continues:

"You know, I don't know why you'd wish to be someone else. You are a *very* beautiful little girl. You always have been," Mr. Kalani says. "When you first came to live with us, your dad was so concerned with getting your room ready because he wanted you to feel at home here. He painted, he bought a bed, he bought toys, he bought a little backpack just for you. Fret, fret, fret. But your uncles were thinking ahead. We said, forget about the room. This girl, she is too beautiful. She's going to fill this lawn with boys. Every night, we're going to have teenage boys on this lawn playing guitars, bringing flowers, reciting poetry. It will be a disaster. So while your dad was getting your room ready, your uncles built that giant fence down at the end of the property and put electric wire up to keep out all your beaus."

I laugh, despite myself.

"That fence is from when the 'mysterious creature' destroyed Dad's whole garden," I say. It was a feral piglet orphan that ended up taking a ride with Animal Control, but Dad refuses to believe that much destruction came from something so small.

"Where do you think the pigs came from? We turned all your suitors into pigs."

I wipe my eyes.

"We missed one. If I see him ever, I'll turn him into bacon," Mr. Kalani says. "Stupid like a pig, that . . . what did you call him?"

"Scumbucket. And anyway, pigs are smart."

"Must not have been as smart as he seemed, sounds like."

Scumbucket told me he liked my curly hair. He said it looked like Myrna Loy's hair when it decided to cooperate. He said he loved it when it dried all funny after swimming in the ocean, because my curls went everywhere and then I looked like a particularly shipwrecked Myrna Loy. While we were dating, I wore it down all the time. I'd get up in the morning, shake it out like Achilles to dry it, and smile in the mirror when I saw it twisting itself every which way. My favorite thing was when he would pull out the spirals without thinking about it while we were tangled up watching movies. But he wanted a straight-haired girl.

"Done," Mr. Kalani announces.

"Thank you, Uncle." I start pulling my hair up into a slobbery wet bun.

"Don't you want some coffee?"

"I'm late," I say. "Got an important workout this morning."

"Oh, wait. That reminds me. I saw a contest to win a bike."

I stop, my hair halfway up.

"What kind of bike?"

"Like the ones in your races."

"Where?"

"In town. You know, next to the clinic that went out of business, where my sister worked in high school."

He's not always very helpful with directions.

He tries again. "Across from the 7-Eleven."

"Half the stores on this island are across from a 7-Eleven."

"The one where Mr. Bu's nephew works. The one on parole."

"Right," I say. I do know where that is.

"You're a lucky girl," Mr. Kalani says. "Maybe you will win."

"Thanks, Uncle. I'll take a look," I say as I throw my bag over my shoulder and head toward my bike. I pull my phone out of my pocket, and I see five messages from Lani on the screen.

"Hey you free this morning?"

"Sucks to ask but can you help out in the truck this morning?"

"You up?"

"I'd ask Trin but she's a disaster with customers."

"Can you text me if you get this? It's kind of an emergency."

I sprint to the house and throw my workout bag back in the front door. I'll have to do that brick another day. The last message was twenty minutes ago. She's probably freaking out.

I head out and text her with one hand as I coast down the hill: "Where? On my way."

~

Last summer when Lani announced that her food truck was going to be called "Fat Girl with a Food Truck," we all tried to tell her that this was a bad idea. "Fat" isn't a dirty word, but even X thought this was going to end up inviting a bunch of shark bait harassing her instead of enjoying her good food. But Lani had a vision.

If there are people making fun of her somewhere out in Twitter land, they don't have the brass to come here. And if they did ever try, there's always a line of loyal customers protecting her like a moat. Today, her line is like half a mile long. I skid up to Fat Girl soaked in sweat, legs burning. I drop my bike and run to the counter. I hear a bunch of "hey"s and angry noises. "She works here," Lani shouts as she hands me her keys with one hand, makes change with the other. The "hey"s turn into cheers, and I turn and take a bow. People literally applaud.

I have a bike lock permanently attached to the back of Lani's trailer, for moments like this when there's nothing sturdy enough to chain it to. I lock up my bike, pull the hidden tarp over it, and climb into the sweltering truck.

"Sorry thank you so much I'm so sorry—"

"Orders or griddle?" I cut her off.

"Orders." I slide in front of the window. "One second, right with you," I tell the first customer.

"What is going on out there?" I ask as I crouch in the corner, changing my shirt with my back to the window. Thank god I was already wearing my sports bra. I put my hair under a cap.

"Some celebrity retweeted the location this morning," Lani says. Her hands are making sandwiches, folding paper around them. "An actor in one of the Marvel movies, I think. I kind of remember him from yesterday, but I didn't know he was famous. But then it went viral and now—"

"Are we going to run out?" I survey the line as I wash my

hands, bag sandwiches, call order numbers. Lani does all her prep at this commercial kitchen where she rents a teeny little space because her mom got tired of her taking over the whole house. The truck is only for putting the food together, not for all the chopping and mixing and measuring. No way we have that much food in here.

"My mom is at the market right now and she's stopping at my fridge," Lani says. She looks like she's about to cry. "What are we going to do? We have to keep this going as long as we can. Normally I'd hang the sign, but, like, this is the best publicity I've ever had. I can't screw this up."

"Roger that," I say, staying super calm and taking an order even though customers are yelling. "Did you text everyone?"

"You're the only one I trust in this kitchen besides me."

I blush a little. Make the change. Think it out. "Order up!" I call, reading off the number.

Lani is a fantastic cook. She's also a great businesswoman. She set this whole thing up herself, permits and all. She is not, however, always the best under pressure. I help Lani out every once in a while with food prep and orders, because I have all the permits and experience from Tua's, so she can leave the truck with me if she has to. But the real reason Lani needs me is that when the lines build up, Lani gets nervous, and then she clams up. Secretly, I think she wants an excuse to shut everything down. And I get that. But I've worked for Tua since I was fourteen. I know how to handle this.

"Okay, real talk?" I say. "Trin's a *rocket scientist.* She can handle orders. We need more hands."

Lani puts the back of her arm over her eyes, thinking.

"I'm doing it." I text the crew before she can argue. X is watching his brothers, Rei's at brunch with her mom, Wyatt has a swim thing, but Trin just might be able to get here. For Lani, she will make it happen.

I lose track of the next hour as I handle this rush and Lani makes sandwich after sandwich.

Finally, Trin is waving in the window. People in line mutter and groan. "She works here!" I shout, and Trin gets a cheer of her own. "Oh, so that's how it is," I shout, and I get a huge laugh. There's not enough room in the truck for all of us, so between orders, I hand her a big platter I've put together with small samples of Lani's amazing taro red bean rolls. They're super pretty with little coconut flakes on them, and they look great on social media, which is exactly where a line of bored tourists is going to put them. I send Trin up and down the line with different samples—a trick I learned from Tua—until morale improves. We don't bother Lani. She's cooking. I'm not even sure she totally knows Trin is here.

Lani's mom shows up in her beat-up car loaded with stuff from Lani's kitchen and the market. Trin helps unload. Some of it isn't right, but it'll do. Lani's mom peeks in the back door, and Lani stops for one second to wave, then goes back to her orders. I know Lani's mom doesn't approve of this. She wants Lani to go to college. But as she's looking at this huge line of people all here to have what her daughter is cooking up, I hope she sees that Lani's got something special. You can always taste it. Today you can see it too. And maybe Lani doesn't need to be good at managing half a mile of hangry people. That's what people like me are for. That's why you need a #supportcrew.

Once the line is calmer, I start Trin on delivering finished orders far away from the truck so there's not such a crowd at the window. And in between, I send her to take as many pictures and videos as she can on Lani's phone with the good camera. People eating, waiting, ordering, smiling. After four hours, we've got the line down to manageable. Lots of people toward the back got samples and left because it was too long. But today's not about making money, though we made freaking bank. It's about getting the word out. Those people will come back some other morning, and hopefully they'll bring their friends.

At two in the afternoon, Trin hangs the OUT OF FOOD sign with much ceremony and we pull down the window.

"Thanks, girls," Lani says, sitting on the stairs outside the truck. She is stained with sweat, totally drained.

"No problem, boss lady. I gotta jet. Makerspace hours," Trin says. She runs away before we can even divvy up the tips.

Lani and I sit in silence for a long time, drinking water and just *being.* A big rush like that can leave your ears ringing. It goes away, but I feel totally filthy and exhausted.

"Thanks," Lani says.

"You already said that."

"Yeah, but you saved the day," Lani says. "And thanks for calling Trinity."

"You have to learn to take help, even if it's not perfect," I say. "Like, what about when you have employees? They're not all going to be as awesome as me. Some of them are going to be dumb."

Lani laughs.

"I don't think Trinity is dumb," she says.

"Not her. But she's not a food person. You have to learn to triage and manage. The food's only half of it."

"Or hire you full-time to do it for me."

"I would never do Tua like that," I say with a smile.

"But for serious. Thanks for being there. Thanks for always being there. And your hair looks nice."

"Thanks," I say sheepishly.

We sit with our exhaustion for a few minutes. I can hear the ocean in the distance. It's like living near a highway in California. After a while, you have to choose to hear it.

At last, Lani clears her throat.

"Can I tell you something and have it be, like, not a big deal?"

"Is it your taro roll recipe? Because that'd be, like, a big deal. And I would totally sell it to Tua for a raise."

She laughs. "Can I tell you something?" she says after a minute.

"Sure."

"Between us?"

"Of course."

"I think I'm gay. Maybe."

"Okay," I say. I'm not surprised. Not really. But why tell me now? Why today? Then it occurs to me. "Oh my god, is it me?"

"No, idiot," Lani says, laughing. "It's not you."

I crinkle my nose at her, very Myrna Loy. It makes me sad for a moment that there's no way she'll get the reference. The only people who do are Scumbucket and X.

"What's wrong with me?" I ask, mock indignant.

"Nothing, it's just not you."

"Fine."

"Are you going to pout?"

"No."

"You're totally pouting. Did you want it to be you?"

"No. But I think you should put some Snickers bars on my nutrition plan to help me save face."

"No dice, babe."

"Twix bars?"

"In what universe is that *better*?"

"Fine. Fine. Let mc guess who it is."

"Who says it has to be a specific person?"

I roll my eyes. I've known for weeks it's *someone.* We all have, I bet. And unless it was a customer, there was only one other person here this morning. Someone who I think of so completely as a feral wolf and a scientist that the fact that she's clearly gay rarely enters my conscious mind.

"Don't guess. It'll make it weird. I don't even know. I definitely don't want to be, like, out or anything. Not in high school. Too much drama. I want it to be a cool thing. A casual thing. I just wanted to try telling someone on for size."

"How was it?"

"Fine." She shrugs. "Kind of just right."

Normally, I think you're supposed to ask all kinds of questions when someone comes out to you. Like, how long have they known? And, are they seeing anyone? And you're definitely supposed to tell the person you totally love them and support them and have this big movie moment of affirmation. But for us, that would be stupid. Lani knows all that.

It's not that complicated.

Still. I don't want her to think I don't care.

"When you come out, will you cater your own party?" I have to ask *something.*

"What?"

"Like, will you have a big coming-out party? I think that's a thing people do. Have you seen debutante balls in old movies? Like *The Reluctant Debutante.*"

"No, because I'm not that kind of gay, you weird, weird thing."

"Good thing I am weird. I know exactly what you do. It's like your gay debutante ball. You're saying, 'Come at me, ladies.' "

I shake my shoulders to demonstrate. She looks at me like I'm an idiot.

"I don't want balloons and a rainbow closet. I think that's how X will come out to his parents someday."

I scoff.

"X will come out to his parents after his very not-gay butler serves them fine cocktails in truly divine Nick and Nora stemware on a tasteful yacht once he buys them a mansion with the fortune he makes as a successful tech millionaire."

"You mean billionaire."

"How much does a yacht cost? Like not a reality TV one but a nice one with wood stuff on it? He was very specific about the wood . . . curvy . . . rail things. You know, that go on stairs."

"You definitely mean banister, and you definitely mean billionaire."

"Whatever. He and I have discussed this extensively. We're going to get engaged beforehand with an absolutely stunning Art Deco sapphire ring, and I'm going to pretend I didn't know he was gay and faint on the deck in my evening gown, and that will distract his parents from the fact that their son is going directly to hell."

"I assume the billions will distract them."

"Or, you know, the fact that they love their son. I did point that out to him."

Lani laughs. I do too. But it's kind of half-hearted. They do love him, but the truth is, we both know the reason X is still basically in the closet and has never had a serious boyfriend (except a sloppy kisser named Patrick who was a total wet noodle) is because we're pretty sure X's dad would totally lose it if he found out. Not even because he's religious. Just because he can't wrap his head around having a gay son.

It's like X says: sometimes people who casually use words like "faggot" surprise you. But more often, they don't. I get that he needs to play his cards right. He needs to play it close to the vest. But sometimes it seems like he plays it so close, he's got this huge person wound up inside him that even I only see glimpses of. And I can't imagine how that feels. He doesn't talk about that kind of thing for serious. Not with anyone. He's out to us. But he's not going to be out for real until he feels like coming out isn't the thing that rips the rug out from under him and ruins his life. After all this waiting, X is going to be a sex maniac when he gets to college, though.

"Don't you ever wish he was more than your best friend?" Lani asks hesitantly. "Two birds with one stone. You guys are so cute together."

She's definitely not asking about me. Not really. I'm not stupid: she wants the analogy to work. But I can't lie either.

"Our thing is different. Like, he's super hot. I totally love him. But that's not our thing. But if our thing changed, I wouldn't be mad or anything. It would just be a different . . . thing."

She stares at me. I totally blew that.

"You know what I mean," I say.

"Do I? Is it something about a 'thing'? I'm a little unclear."

"All I'm saying is, just because someone is your best friend doesn't mean they don't want to date you. But it also doesn't mean that being best friends isn't great also."

"Yeah," she says, looking downcast.

"Is it your parents?" I ask.

"Not exactly. My parents aren't like X's. They won't care. Not like that. But they'll want to make a big thing of it, like announce it to their friends and do a whole 'divorced parents united front we hate each other but we still love you' song and dance. They'd definitely want your coming-out party. So I want to be way the hell gone before I tell them. Just, like, show up at Thanksgiving with a girl or something. If I decide I'm gay and all."

"Your mom seemed so proud of you when she stopped by."

Lani smiled. "She's just my mom, but having her do something like that? Actually show up when I needed her? I don't know. It matters."

"Yeah," I say, because I get what she's saying. It's like, your parents can say they love you all the time, but there's something about when they pick you up when you need them the most that reminds you they matter in a way no one else ever will.

"I still wish she believed in me enough to let me do this for real. She thinks it's just a hobby. Like I'm playing chef and it's an elaborate lemonade stand."

I shake my head. "Not today she didn't. No one thought that today."

Lani looks over her shoulder into her truck, and for a second she just stares.

"I know," she says at last. "Not even me."

chapter thirteen

It takes two hours of bus and bike to get to Ala Moana, even with Lani dropping me off on her way home. When I finally get there, I head toward the enormous food court, bobbing and weaving through the crowds. Everyone has sharp-edged paper bags with string handles and fancy brand names on the front. No plastic bags here. Some girls have whole garlands of them hanging off their arms. They swipe my bare legs as I walk by.

I make it through the basic bitch obstacle course and to the food court. I slide into a plastic chair and take a breath. I am so tired. I don't know why I'm tired. I didn't even do my workout.

I want to put my head down, but I don't want to get picked up by a guard for loitering. Instead, I buy a cheeseburger and make myself eat it while I wait.

Ala Moana is a ginormous mall. For me it might as well be an open-air museum of stuff I'll never have. I've got today's tips in my pocket, and it almost feels like I could afford to shop here.

I come here with Rei a lot. Rei loves to try on clothes. She doesn't even buy that much stuff, she just likes seeing herself in different outfits. She doesn't mind if I tell her a dress makes her legs look short. She knows how to fix that with heels or a hem.

I don't know how to fix anything. I care about how I look, sure. But I care in the sense that I have a jean jacket I sewed a bunch of patches on that I love. I care in that all my T-shirts are for bands and books I could not function without. I like to like my clothes. I never like them on me.

"Miho!"

I look up. It's Rei's mom, waving from across the food court. I wave back; then she gives Rei a kiss and walks away. Rei walks toward me, a brown bag hanging from the crook of her arm. Post-brunch shopping with her mom.

I watch Rei sashay across the food court. I watch eyes follow her. I look down and brush the crumbs off my shirt.

"Was that your ride?" I ask.

"We took two cars," she explains as she slides into the seat across from me. "We can put your bike in the back on the way home."

She looks me over.

"Did you bike here?" she asks.

"Part of the way."

"This outfit," Rei says. I look down at my extra-baggy shirt and pants so roomy they pull right off my hips.

"Easy to get on and off," I explain, polishing off my burger and crumpling up the wrapper. "I still don't see what's wrong with wearing sweatpants to work out."

"Nothing's *wrong* with it. They're just wrong for what you're doing."

"I bike all the time in sweatpants."

"Mi-kins. Trust me. You should look as good as you feel."

"That sounds like a sex thing."

"Is Trinity rubbing off on you? It's not a sex thing."

"That's what she said."

"You're trying to annoy me out of shopping for you. But it won't work. You said we could buy you some real workout clothes, and you're not backing out. We're gonna put racing stripes up and down those lightning legs."

"You mean thunder thighs."

"I mean light-up-the-road, shock-the-competition lightning legs. And we're going matchy-matchy."

"No."

"Oh yes. Full tracksuit. You're going to be adorable."

"No."

"If you think matchy-matchy is as bad as triathlon fashion gets, I have got some bad news for you."

"You can put my cold, dead corpse in a matching tracksuit."

"Anything is possible."

Soon I'm standing behind one of those slatted doors in a store I did not know existed before today, staring down a garment that has five holes and one zipper.

"Put it on," Rei says.

"I don't know how."

"It's just like a romper."

"What is a romper?"

"It's like a jumpsuit."

"But is this the front or the back?"

"I'm coming in."

"No! I'll do it, I'll do it."

I wrangle myself into the *thing* while listening to Rei sing the same four bars of "Wouldn't It Be Loverly" over and over, perfecting some tiny note or tremor that mere mortals can't even hear.

I want to ask her about her play. I want to ask her about Wyatt. That's how this usually goes. She talks, I listen. She dresses, I critique. She's behind the door, and I'm out there waiting. That's the way I like it.

I open the door.

"I would rather die," I say as the song leaves her lips and she spins around, her eyes lighting up.

"And I will shove your adorable corpse into it."

"Why do they wear these things?" I ask, looking at myself in the mirror. It has sleeves, kind of, and shorts, kind of, and it's all one piece with the world's biggest pad sewn right into the crotch. But the shorts are too tight, and the sleeves are too loose, and none of it looks right.

"It's all for speed. It's called a trisuit question mark?" Rei says. She looks me over again, shaking her head. "This doesn't fit, but you're going to look like a superhero when we find you one that does. Although we're going to have to discuss the, uh, matter of unmentionables."

"If it's unmentionable, why are you mentioning it?" I ask. My stomach is tied in knots.

"Mi-kins, look at your butt in the mirror," Rei says.

I turn around. There's a clear outline of my Hanes granny panties.

"Internet says: no underwear, yes bra," Rei informs me.

"I say no to all of it," I say, covering my face in my hands.

Rei sighs with the full force of the Stanislavski method.

She takes me by the shoulders and turns me to the mirror. "Listen, Queen. You're right. The very, very first one we looked at doesn't look great. But so what? That's the joy of shopping. It's *never* right the first time. Remember how many stores we scoured to find my sweet sixteen dress? We're treasure hunting."

I say nothing. I bet Rei would look great in this trisuit. I'm not thinking of Rei, though. I'm thinking of *her,* with her perfect flat stomach, wearing a pink version of this on Instagram, two fingers in a V.

"So what do you like about it?" Rei asks.

"Nothing."

"Miho," she growls.

I want to take this off and pretend none of this ever happened. But I look at Rei. She points to the mirror.

I think: maybe I need Rei now, like Lani needed me this morning. Maybe Rei is my fashion #supportcrew.

I try to look only at the clothes in the mirror, and not at myself, the way you can take apart anything you draw into lines and colors.

"What about the design? Do you like these squiggles?" Rei prompts. I can tell even she doesn't like the squiggles, but she doesn't want to color my judgment.

"No," I decide. "I'm firmly anti-squiggle. But . . ." I think about it. "Well, I do wish it had more decorations on it."

"What kind of decorations?" Rei has her phone out, googling.

"Like maybe a bird or something? Or sunflowers?"

"You and your sunflowers."

"Or maybe if it wasn't just plain black," I say. I lift my arms up and down. I try to imagine what this would feel like, riding on my bike. Fine, I guess, on the bike. But for swimming? "And I wish it didn't have sleeves."

"What *do* you like about it?"

I spin around in the mirror. I discover something at the exact location of a tramp stamp. I zip it open, then closed again.

"So the butt pocket's a winner," Rei says.

"I don't need to work out in this, though?" I ask, halfway between pleading and a question.

"No, of course not. I mean, you can. People do. But you don't have to. You don't even have to have a one-piece one if you don't like it."

I look in the mirror again. *She wears one,* whispers something in the back of my mind.

"Maybe." I try not to think about it. "If we found the right one, it wouldn't be too bad."

We move on to workout clothes. When we finally find a matching leggings and top with racing stripes on the legs that Rei likes, and I agree would look nice on someone else, we go to the register and I pull out my handful of cash.

"I've got this," Rei says as she hands over her Amex. "It's an early birthday present."

I put my money away. Money is always a little weird with Rei.

"Don't worry, you're going to need to buy plenty of stuff," Rei says as we leave the store. "But this is special. This is your power costume."

"Power costume?"

"Every girl should have a power costume," Rei says. "Mine is this sparkly Adidas tennis set. I wear it for like half of hell week."

Rei says things like this sometimes, these things I think she reads in *Teen Vogue* or whatever magazine tells her how to make her hair board-straight. "Every girl should" or "All girls must." Sometimes it's like she's reading out of the secret girl rule book that all girls have but me. And sometimes it's like she's trying way too hard.

I loop my very own paper bag over my arm. We stroll until we get to the big spotty pumpkin sculpture that sits in a fountain. It's a Yayoi Kusama. I imagine Mrs. Miller's brain exploding: What does it mean when a sculpture is a pumpkin?

We take a seat. I peer into the bag while Rei texts . . . probably Wyatt, judging by the smile on her face.

"Okay, what's next?" Rei asks as she slides away her phone. "Run stuff? Swimsuit?"

I shift. "I think I should probably just, you know, stick with what I have. Like, my gym clothes are fine."

"Serious question, Miho. Do you own *any* running clothes?"

"I have sweatpants."

"Do you have a sports bra?"

"Maybe? Is this one a sports bra?"

I pull my shirt forward and she looks down my collar.

"No, Miho, that's a bralette. Or maybe a trainer bra. Where did you even get that?"

"It was in the three-pack my dad bought me when I turned thirteen."

"Please tell me you haven't been wearing that since you were thirteen."

"Okay, I'm not telling you that I've been wearing it since I was thirteen."

Rei sighs.

"And a bathing suit?" she asks.

"You've seen all my swimsuits."

"You can't do a triathlon in a tankini with the elastic half melted," she says. "If you have to buy all new stuff anyway, why not buy clothes that make you feel fancy and fast?"

"Because it will look ridiculous on me," I say, looking into the bag. "I mean, this will be fun to wear, but it'll be like a costume."

"All clothes are costumes," Rei says. She grabs my shoulders and shakes me. "That. Is. The. Point. You get to choose the costume."

I consider that. "Okay."

"Plus, you're turning eighteen this year. You're allowed to reinvent yourself. It's in the official adulthood blood covenant the devil makes you sign when he comes through your window at midnight on your birthday."

"That's not a thing."

"It's totally a thing. Although I'll probably be getting a visit from Satan tonight since it's explicitly forbidden to tell anyone who isn't eighteen yet."

"You're hilarious."

"Seriously. Keep your window open on your birthday. Do *not* make Satan knock."

I laugh, and try to make it sound happy.

"What is it?" Rei asks.

I shrug.

"Come on."

"My birthday is kind of ruined," I say.

"How is it ruined? It's in July."

"Yeah, but it was a special thing. Between me and . . . Scumbucket."

My face gets red.

"Oh! I totally forgot. I gave you that silly lingerie from *Cabaret* so you could wear it for him."

Rei had worn the set for two different shows—*Cabaret* and *West Side Story*. If we'd been less close, I would have been grossed out by the idea of putting fabric that had directly covered her nether orifices all up in my own. But we're close enough that I would wear Rei's underwear secondhand without too much squeamishness; I've done so on several impromptu sleepovers.

The lingerie was two pieces that kind of looped together with buttons. Lavender, in a weird satiny fabric with lace and bows. And unlike normal sexy-ish bras that turn your boobs into molded Barbie-lumps, it left everything kind of hanging out under a thin band of lace. It had straps and stuff, but it was more decorative than technical. The bottom half was designed for someone like Rei, with a bit more in the butt department. On me, I thought it looked kind of like satin gym shorts, even though Rei said it looked better on me than on her. I felt ridiculous. Until he told me I looked beautiful. Until he looked at me, and I could see he really believed it.

Then I felt exactly the way you're supposed to feel when you wear that kind of thing. I felt, for once, like I was worth everything that any man has to give.

"But why is your birthday ruined?" Rei asks, snapping me back to the present.

"We had this plan. It seems stupid now."

"Tell me."

I sigh. "Last year, we spent the night out on the beach, right? And he said that *this* year, since I'd be turning eighteen, we'd run away and go to Amsterdam together for a week and go to the Van Gogh Museum. His grandfather promised him a bunch of money for a graduation trip, and he was going to take me. He said he couldn't 'find himself' without me. He kept talking about it like it would really happen, all through last fall, all through the winter. He would send me little things we were adding to 'The Itinerary.' He gave me his *Lonely Planet,* and I'd send him things I wanted to make sure we did. Down to, like, specific rooms at the Rijksmuseum, which is truly massive. Down to which of our favorite movies we'd watch on the flights. He picked the hotel. He penciled in the best rijsttafel restaurant he'd ever been to. I could taste this trip, I swear. And he had it all written out in his Moleskine, this hour-by-hour plan starting at midnight on my birthday."

"Wow. I know he's a bucket of scum, but . . ."

"Yeah, it was the cutest thing ever."

"Except for the Scumbucket part."

"Yeah. Anyway, we were adding things to 'The Itinerary' right up until he broke up with me. And now, when it's my birthday, it's going to be like those hours are ticking by, and I'll know exactly what should have been happening in each of them."

"You could still go."

"Yeah, right."

"Why not?"

"I don't know. I'm just . . . not the kind of person who does those kind of things."

"Don't be ridiculous. You know literally everything about that ear-chopping weirdo."

"I can't afford it."

"Maybe your dad would help? Graduation gift?"

I pause. I don't even want to think about what Rei is getting for a graduation gift. She got a brand-new Prius for her sixteenth birthday.

It's like this never quite computes for Rei. She abstractly understands that I'm poor. She sees it in my house, my clothes, but she still doesn't *get* it. And she says these things without thinking about them. Like how when I told her I was sick of using the computers at the public library, she told me I should just "ask for a laptop." Or today, how she didn't even see how incredible it is that her family has *three* cars, so she and her mom could take *two* of them for a shopping trip without having to shuffle everyone around. It took me two hours to get to this mall. It took her thirty minutes, tops.

She's not trying to be mean. I know that. But god she's tone-deaf sometimes.

"My dad can't afford to send me on a vacation to Europe," I say.

"But you're an artist! It's not a vacation, it's education."

"Yeah, but even for school . . . I mean, that's why Trinity didn't do that summer program at Carnegie Mellon last year even though she got in. Her parents couldn't afford it even *with* the financial aid."

I stop myself from saying anything more. Rei went to theater camp every summer in New York growing up, and I can tell I'm making her feel bad.

Rei and Scumbucket have this in common: they don't like to be reminded of how well-off they are. The few times we hung out together in a big group, it was like seeing another rich person made them feel accused of something. They'd try to "out-poor" each other, mentioning things that they *didn't* have: private tutors, luxury clothes. They'd make fun of other rich kids they knew, who flew on private planes and were afraid of being kidnapped. It was super awkward, like they had to prove they belonged with the rest of us.

But when it was just me, Rei, and Scumbucket, the "poorer than thou" competition calmed way down, and we had a lot of fun together. Sometimes I wondered if it was too much fun. I didn't like the way they made jokes about the bad service they'd had on different international airlines, because I didn't get it. I didn't like how their dads belonged to rival golf clubs, or how their moms both spent too much time at the same luxury nail salon that served mimosas all day. I didn't like how they understood each other.

I was jealous.

"It doesn't matter anyway because I wanted to go with him," I say, to break the silence. "We were supposed to see those things together. He told me my birthday was his favorite holiday."

"You two were weird. Was Scumbucket the first guy you slept with?"

I shift uncomfortably and gaze upon the pumpkin. Rei is my best girlfriend, but I've only ever talked about this kind of thing with X. I'm not even 100 percent sure if Rei has had sex. She's super cagey about it.

"So that's a yes," Rei says. "Was that the first time? Your birthday?"

"No. The first time was in this mansion he was housesitting. We watched all the *Thin Man* movies in a row, and we just kept doing it, like over and over. My birthday was . . ."

"What?"

"I guess it's when I realized he was the person I wanted to be with forever." My voice cracks. "I'm so stupid. I believed we'd be together forever."

"Yeah," Rei says, wrapping her arm around me.

"I feel so dumb," I say, laughing.

"You're not dumb. Look, don't tell anyone, but I think I really like Wyatt. Like, maybe love him?"

"Ew, gross," I say. She laughs, sticks her tongue out at me.

"I hope he's not gonna do me like Scumbucket did you."

"Oh, hc wouldn't. Wyatt's good people," I say. And guys probably don't do that to girls like Rei.

"You and Wyatt are friends in that game you play, right?" she asks, a little too casually.

"Yeah, but he's never on," I say. "I think he added me to be nice. Scumbucket was my only friend."

"But that's what I'm saying. *Who knows* who Wyatt talks to on there. Or on his phone. You'd never know. The only thing you can do is trust him, because cheaters get caught. Especially dumb ones like Scumbucket."

I nod.

"Too bad Wyatt isn't dumb," Rei says. "I'd never know."

Scumbucket wasn't dumb either.

"I wish you'd tell her," Rei says. "Think of him as a dad cheating on her in PlayStation Land, having affairs on his phone while she's having their second kid, their third. I couldn't stand it, knowing I'd been two-timed. I feel for you. But I feel for her too."

I know exactly what she means. I kind of think I'm breaking the girl code by not telling her. She deserves to know the truth. But it's not only about her. It's about their kid.

My dad left my mom and me before I was born. But my mom had a lot of problems of her own. Maybe it was hard, being a single parent. But one day, she just . . . broke. I don't know if it was drugs, or stress, or if she was just a bad person. But she picked me up from school one day, drove halfway home, stopped on the side of the road, told me to get out, and then drove away and never came back. I was in sixth grade. I stood on the highway with my lunch box and my little backpack for what felt like days. The cars rushed by. Finally, the police picked me up. I went to the police station. They found my dad, somehow. And then my memory kind of blacks out, and I was here. I refused to get in cars for months. Maybe that's why I like my bike so much.

I could never be the reason that kid's mom dumps her on the side of the road and vanishes. I could never be the reason that kid's dad decides to bounce before she's even born. It doesn't matter if your dad comes back for a World's Best Dad third act after your mom abandons you, and then you're sitting in a police station in California so terrified that you wet yourself. He still left.

"Anyway, you know, just because he was first, doesn't mean

he was best," she says. "This is a small pond. There will be other Scumbuckets."

"I hope not."

"I mean other . . . what did you used to call him? 'Partners in crime.' There will be other loves, but this one is going to hurt for a while."

"But what if the person I love doesn't want me?"

"Then you'll find another."

"But what if it's me? What if I'm not what that kind of person wants?"

She raises an eyebrow.

"What?"

"I mean . . . what if the kind of guy I am destined to fall in love with only wants . . ."

I look around, looking for a way to say it. I spot a J. Crew down a passageway.

"What if that kind of guy only wants *that* kind of girl?" I ask, pointing to J. Crew.

"What kind of girl?"

"That one. And that one. And that one," I say as I watch a few girls from St. Agatha's going into the store. They're all wearing uniforms for some team.

"That's not a *kind* of girl. Those are all just girls shopping at J. Crew."

"Yeah, but I couldn't shop there."

"Why?"

"You know I can't afford it."

"Yes you can. You just don't want to spend stupid amounts of money on clothes."

"Fine. I can't shop there because those clothes would look ridiculous on someone like me."

"Now, *that* is a ridiculous thing to say. And I'm sick of hearing it."

Rei grabs my arm and heads toward the store.

"Wait," I say, pulling back in panic. Rei is stronger.

"You did this to yourself. It's time to face the horror of J. Crew."

~

Rei wanders around, picking things up. I shadow her so closely I step on her foot.

"Ow!" says Rei.

"Do you need any help?" asks one of the clerks. Rei examines her foot, and I stare at the salesgirl like a deer in headlights. She's the same age as us, and seems more bored than judgmental.

"Yeah, sale rack?" Rei asks. The girl points us upstairs, then heads off.

"Can we leave?" I ask.

"No," says Rei. "We're going to find those girls."

We pass through the men's section, and I spot the pink linen shirt that Scumbucket left with me. I slept in it for a week once when he was on vacation. I wonder which one his real girlfriend was sleeping in. Rei is dramatically limping up the stairs away from me, and I follow her. The St. Agatha's girls are on the other side of the store, and they don't notice us. We watch them sideways as we pick through the sale rack. I look at the price on a plain skirt. It's ten dollars.

"Oh," I say. "How is this so cheap?"

"Fast fashion is killing the planet," Rei says, shaking her head. "When they do sales here, they basically give it away. How do you think X affords all those ridiculous button-downs and chinos?"

I never thought about it. The St. Agatha's girls let out a peal of laughter.

"The difference between you and those girls is this"—she pulls a skirt off the sale rack— "this, this, and this"—she throws a shirt, some tights, and a pair of chunky heels my way—"and twenty minutes with some mascara and a flat iron," Rei says.

"That sounds like a lot."

"That's the price of three pizzas."

"Yeah, okay, fine. Even if I dressed like them, I wouldn't *be* like them. It's like I said. It'd be a costume."

"That's what clothes are. If you don't get it by now, Miho, it's because you don't want to get it," Rei says. She slides a velvet headband with little pearls on it over my hair, floofs it out to the side. I look in the little face mirror posted on the table.

And for the first time I see it: this one tiny slice of me could look like someone else. Could *be* someone else.

She's right. We're in a J. Crew and no one is even looking at us. *This time,* whispers my brain. Just because you got away with it once doesn't mean you always will. I've been followed in a store before. That stuff happens. But this time? It's nice.

I take the headband off, pile it up with everything else. A Coke with my three pizzas. "Should I buy it?" I ask awkwardly, nodding to the clothes.

"Do you like them?"

"No."

"Then no. Obviously. But you could."

I look over again at the girls we followed in. They're so effortlessly clean, their hair shiny and neat.

"Look," Rei says. "Let me prove it to you. If I can turn myself into a green witch"—*Wicked.* She was phenomenal—"I can turn you into one of them. If you walk the walk, everyone will assume that's the way you always walk."

I nod.

"So? Are you ready to walk the walk?" Rei asks. I dump the clothes back on the table.

"There will be pizza?" My stomach growls.

"And makeup! And hair! And a dramatic chair-spin reveal in front of my mom's vanity!"

"And also pizza?"

"And also pizza," she says.

~

When I get home, I run to my room and look at myself in the long, tall mirror. I'm wearing the running clothes that Rei bought me, with one of Rei's open-back mesh shirts layered over it. With my shirt tied in a little knot and my hair straight, I look so different. Rei was right: a flat iron and some mascara. I look like I don't belong in my own room.

I straighten myself up, flip my hair, stand at just the right angle so it almost looks like I have a thigh gap. I look just like them.

"What are you doing?"

I crumple.

"Dad!" I shout. I forgot to close the door.

"Modeling?"

"No. What are *you* doing?" He is wearing his hook leg, and I want to ask him why, but I'm too embarrassed. He looks sheepish. Also sweaty. Was he running?

"I asked you first," he says.

"Rei gave me a makeover."

He raises an eyebrow. I sigh loudly.

"You look . . . nice. I know these are very trendy, but they are not pants."

"Dad. They're leggings."

"Why exactly are you wearing them and where are you going in them? Surely not out of this room."

"I'm just trying them on, okay? They're for running," I snap. He raises his hands, laughing.

"As long as it's not to school. Dinner in fifteen minutes. Did you eat?"

"No," I lie. Somehow I'm hungry again. He shuts the door still grinning. I can't be mad. He didn't mean anything by it.

I take it off and shove everything in a drawer.

chapter fourteen

Two months pass in a blaze of schoolwork and training and work and training and friends and training and training and training. I barely notice prom, yearbooks, senior pranks. It's all white noise. Rei and Wyatt make a cute prom couple. Lani and Trin go, *not as a couple,* but "maybe as a couple," each one tells me secretly. They refuse to talk to each other about it, so I tag along. This way no one has to admit that they have feelings for anyone, even though it's painfully obvious. They dance all night, leaving me to fantasy-shop for bikes on my phone under the sparkle of a disco ball. I dream of speed all evening. Trin and Lani do not hook up, or confess their mutual attraction, despite my best efforts. X takes his cousin to his swanky prom so his mom's heart won't be broken and she'll get her prom photos. He doesn't ask me, and of course I know why. Instead of going to the afterparty, he comes over to my place to binge-watch *The Avengers.* He lets me keep his bow tie.

I run in the dark before school. I find out that not only does my school have a gym, but apparently, I've been able to use it this whole time. It's not limited to team sport athletes and PE classes. So I splash water on my face at five a.m., and I'm in the building at six a.m. every school day, logging miles on the rickety treadmills with the judo boys and the softball girls. We avoid each other for a few days, until we start arguing about what to watch on the single TV. I'm on Team *X-Files*. We hate Team Food Network. And then on the basis of television preferences, I find myself with a new crew I never would have talked to at school.

I ride the spin bikes. It's like having a genie who can take me anywhere, to ride any terrain I want: steep hills and flat stretches I could never find outside. I never imagined I'd enjoy riding a bike that goes nowhere, but now I can choose my workout instead of taking what I can find. I can work only one leg (my left is lazy), spin high RPMs to build "fast-twitch muscles," or simply enjoy not worrying about getting hit by a car as I push myself past my threshold. In April, Mr. Smith, the weight room monitor, pulls me aside, and I think I'm in trouble, but he wants to show me how to use the cable machines, because "Strength complements cardio." He remembers me from when I took non-optional gym in ninth grade, and I'm shocked. I thought he didn't even know my name. He says, "Of course I remember you. You're the passive-resistance basketball player." He gives me weight-training sheets to fill out and file in a folder with all the other kids. I watch the numbers go up and I love it. I can do a pull-up. Just one. But still. My *X-Files* posse cheers so loud when I finally do it that the band kids down the hall complain. I barely get my chin to the bar, but I feel like a superhero.

I swim after school when I have a long enough break between school and work. I'm worried about the 2.4-mile swim, even though I'm practicing everything like I should. It just seems so far. Right now, it takes me an hour and twenty minutes and I can't get faster. I've plateaued. Some days, when Wyatt doesn't practice with his team, we swim together. I make fun of his ridiculous swim drills, which are all named after inanimate objects and performed like math problems: Eggbeater Drill for 4 x 50. 4 x 25 on :30. Tape Dispenser Drill x 300. Hold your hands like this, lift your elbows, stop breathing weird! Sometimes X comes and cheers us on while he does homework. Sometimes we meet alone and just swim, split a lane, with his much crazier set printed out on a piece of paper and stuck to a wet kickboard. I tell him it looks like a tombstone that reads, "This is what killed our dear friend Wyatt."

And soon, I don't get faster, but it does get easier. I must be doing something right.

And of course I run. I'm terrified of the marathon, but I watch the distance go up every week on my long runs. Five miles. Ten miles. A half marathon and I didn't even cry! I remember when I couldn't even run three miles. Now I can run fifteen. Well, walk and run. It's a strategy, though: run .9, walk .1. But I can do better. I know it. I'm going to run the whole thing.

I log twenty hours a week of training on some weeks, if you count pizza deliveries. At first I'm half-asleep at school, but then, after a few weeks, I'm wide-awake. It's like I'm flying. I'm sore everywhere, but I'm also weirdly happy all the time. Having absolutely no time makes me organized. I have lists of everything that needs to get done. I zip through my homework, my chores. I haven't thought about that Scumbucket or his fiancée in weeks. I know they're getting married soon, but I don't care, not at all. I don't have time to worry or be sad. There's no time to think. I just do what has to get done.

By the time May rolls around, I'm a machine.

chapter fifteen

"Delivery!" Uncle Tua shouts. I lift myself painfully off the kitchen floor, where I've been half cleaning, half dozing.

The address looks a little familiar, but it's not one of my regulars. I waste the data on Google Maps to narrate the trip so I don't screw up the directions—I'm that tired. The past few weeks have been awful. Everything was going great, and then all of a sudden, the harder I train, the worse I get. I can't think.

As I'm biking, all I can think about is how hungry I am. Delivering pizzas after my run or my swim or doing intervals on the bike on top of school on top of freaking *everything else* I have to do, there's no amount of food that seems to help. I realize pedal by pedal that I have to eat, even though I already had dinner. Lani said this might happen, so I have a snack with me at all times, unless I've already eaten it. I don't even stop my bike. I don't have time. I open my sandwich and ride without my hands on the handlebars as I cram it into my mouth. I am so hungry I can barely see. This triathlon has taken over my whole life.

I make myself remember: I'm choosing this. I *want* to do this. Sure, I felt terrible a minute ago, but it's a good terrible because it's making me stronger. And I feel a little better after a few bites of food.

It's scary how something like hunger can change how you think about yourself. I don't think I really understood hunger until I started training.

I came close back when I lived with my mom. She lost her job and we were broke. I was on a free meal program at school, and I felt so lucky and so scared. Lucky, because we still had enough to eat. Scared, because there were kids who clearly didn't. Sitting around those big white cafeteria tables, the kids next to me didn't always look different than me, but some of them ate like they knew they weren't getting another chance.

Even in elementary school, we all knew better than to tell the others, the ones who weren't at breakfast. We had fun, played games, and talked. But there was this unspoken rule: what happens at breakfast stays at breakfast. At lunch, everyone had a swipe card, so no one knew where your lunch was coming from. But before school, corralled together, we were vulnerable. We knew it, even if we didn't have a name for it. We knew what the food meant, and that we should all be ashamed. I can't imagine being *truly* hungry, like I am now, on top of that.

My grandfather started driving up to visit a lot, like every single week, and he would buy us a ton of groceries, lots of vegetables, but treats too, and it was the best thing ever because we had Nutella and brand-name cereal and all the best frozen stuff from Trader Joe's. Looking back, I think that he was trying to get my mom into rehab, or maybe back on her meds. I wish I knew what really happened, but there's no one left to ask. I remember them fighting a lot, and sometimes my mom would yell at him until he left, and then she'd yell at me for crying about it. At least I had someone. Not everyone has that. I can't imagine how much it must have sucked to be those hungry kids at school. This kind of hunger makes it so you can't think. It's the kind of hunger that makes you stop on the side of the road and beat up a vending machine trying to get a Snickers, even though Lani told you not to eat any more candy because candy is not food. I mean, who would do that. Only a lunatic. But hunger makes you stupid. When I feel that hunger now, I have literally eaten abandoned pizza off customers' plates as I take them to the kitchen sink.

Maybe that's the difference between hungry and hunger. Hungry is what you feel before dinner. Hunger is what you fear.

I could be that hungry again but without the choice. I could go to college, get a useless degree in art and lots of debt, and find myself on food stamps with no way out. Or maybe I'd be successful for a little while and then one thing would go wrong and I would plummet out of the sky. I have a pretty okay life right now. I could deliver pizzas forever, maybe even take over from Tua someday, and never have to worry about food. Why would I risk what I have? If I fly too close to the sun, there's not a whole lot my dad will be able to do to help me.

I could be hungry for the rest of my life.

"Your destination is on the left," my phone announces. I skid to a stop. I'm here, but I don't remember listening. I wipe my mouth on my sleeve and leave a trail of Lani's fancy sandwich spread. Whatever. I grab the pizzas, walk up to the gate, and ring the intercom.

"Pizza delivery from Uncle Tua's for . . ." I look at the slip of paper. "Sailor Chibi Moon?"

God I hope this isn't a prank. That's all I need tonight.

Someone buzzes me in. As I walk toward the front door, I realize I do know where I am. I can't place it. It's only a medium-sized mansion in this neighborhood, but it still seems huge to me.

I ring the doorbell. I hear footsteps coming toward the door, so I smile my biggest smile and straighten up. The door opens and—

And.

And.

The smile doesn't fall off my face. The pizzas don't fall out of my hands.

"Ladies, the pizza's here!" she calls over her shoulder. She is wearing a Sailor Moon tiara that has "Bride" written on it in glitter ink.

I hear the "woo" before I see them. They appear from down a hallway, walking strangely on those toe separator things.

They're all wearing matching pink satin robes over pink bathing suits. She's obviously pregnant but still looks perfect. I don't even sense the pizzas lift out of my hands. I'm still smiling, staring at her like an idiot.

"Daddy, where's your wallet?" she calls into the house.

"By the door," a disembodied voice calls back. "Tell him to keep the change."

She thumbs through the wallet.

"On a hundred?" she calls back.

"If that's all there is," he replies.

She turns back to me, leafing through the wallet. Not once has she even looked at me as a person. A uniform makes you invisible.

"Your lucky day!" she says, not even noticing that I haven't said anything. She hands me a hundred-dollar bill and I feel my hand take it. Then she shuts the door, and I listen as the woos go down the hallway away from the door.

My legs carry me back to my bike. My hand puts the hundred-dollar bill in my pocket, and I force myself to ride away. My eyes turn to the side of the house as I coast away, and there, in the back, I can see it now.

There's the pool house.

~

As I bike back to Tua's, I'm so furious my brain shorts out and I make a wrong turn. All the "getting over him" I thought I'd done over the last few months. I'm so stupid. Why can't I turn love off? Why is it sitting here, in my chest, fueling this flame that's doing nothing for me?

Sometimes, the universe just sucker punches you.

I *have* been to her house before. Or rather, her pool house, site of the *Thin Man* movie marathon.

He cheated on her *in her own house.*

I should be righteously angry, but I just feel . . . I don't know.

Why am I so easy to forget? Why am I someone who can be thrown away by a dad, by a mom, and by my partner in crime? Things that seem so permanent, people who seem so solid, they . . . vanish. And they never look back. Will my friends remember me after this year? Am I even someone worth remembering?

My pedal strokes become a chant: The Little Engine That Hated Herself.

I hate myself. I hate myself. I hate myself.

Just like there's hungry and hunger, there's sad and this pain I don't have a name for. The thing you fear. But there's nothing I can do.

I pull up to Tua's. I walk briskly but calmly through the completely full restaurant. *Keep it together,* I tell myself. I grab my stuff out of my employee locker, then hand Uncle Tua the hundred-dollar bill. He looks at the bill, then at me.

"I'm not feeling well Uncle Tua I'm really sorry I need to go can you clock me out," I say all at once. I try to keep it together, but the second I open my mouth, tears start falling. I head back out the door as quickly as I can. I walk into a chair that screeches across the floor, but no one looks up. I have to get away. I am choking on sobs and so embarrassed. The customers don't notice, but Uncle Tua follows me out front.

"Miho, what's wrong?"

"Nothing, I just. I just."

I can't even answer. I'm sobbing, and I have to go. He reaches out to grab my hand, but I pull away.

"Miho, your tips!"

I pedal away as fast as I can.

chapter sixteen

Two weeks later, I get off work on Friday and instead of hanging out with my friends, I play *Eldritch Codex* all night. I'm pretending to look for the Stone of Hermes, but I'm honestly just sneaking around the places I used to haunt with Scumbucket. I'm surprised he hasn't been online this whole time. He's the one who got me hooked on this game in the first place.

I've been doing this kind of a lot. I even blew off a few training runs to play. I still want to do this race, but the more training I blow off, the easier it is to just . . . not. The spark is gone.

If I could get myself together, maybe it would come back.

I promise myself. Tomorrow. I will get back to training tomorrow. This is the last night of moping. Hard stop.

The light from my phone gets my attention. I realize I've played all through the night. It's getting light out. I haven't slept at all.

It's a text from X.

"Are you up?" he writes. I switch off the PlayStation and text a thumbs-up.

"Put some pants on and grab your swim stuff," he writes. "I'm outside."

I sigh. Normally, I'd be bursting with excitement for this kind of early morning adventure. Today, I want to crawl into bed.

Suck it up, I tell myself. I slap a smile on my face, put on my swimsuit with a dress over it. I stuff a towel, cap, and goggles into my backpack. What else would a happy Miho choose to pack? I look at my sketchbook. I leave it on the floor.

I close my bedroom door, shush Achilles, leave Dad a note in the kitchen, and hop into the car.

"You look like hell," X says.

"That's what you get when you rush a lady," I reply, trying to muster some banter. "Where are we going?"

He tells me about how he joined the Waikiki Swim Club Facebook page, and how he got a tip on a great swimming beach. We're going to have to drive, though. It's an hour and a half away, the other side of the island.

"So it's a workout?" I ask, a little deflated.

He shrugs. "Rei added a makeup session since you got so behind last week," he says. "Unless you're having second thoughts about this whole Ironman thing."

"No." I try to sound more confident than I feel. "Burn rubber."

This is a real open-ocean swim. Not a snorkeling trip, not messing around in the perfect Hawaiian surf. A swim. For miles. I watch bubbles streaming from my fingertips with each stroke, listen to the sound of myself gasping for breath. There are beautiful fish. X said there's even a shipwreck somewhere down there, supposedly. And sharks, but I try not to think about that. There's so much to see under the water. But all I'm seeing is my own slow pace. All I'm feeling is the burning salt water that keeps getting in my nose as I try to sight.

I stop. I paddle over and cling to the kayak for dear life, trying to catch my breath.

"You're not even trying," X says. He looks at some app on his phone. "We've only gone a mile."

Over half an hour to swim a mile. *Ridiculous,* I think to myself. I've been biking slower too. I tell my legs, "Get yourselves together!" but even though it feels like I'm working as hard as I possibly can, like my RPE is freaking eleven, I'm slower and slower day by day. I've been exhausted ever since I delivered that pizza. I thought it was the missed training, but maybe I'm just a garbage triathlete.

I take off my goggles. X looks at his watch. "You need to keep going. If we sit here and let your heart rate fall, you won't get the benefits—"

"Will you give me a break? There wasn't even a swim on the calendar today."

"I told you. Rei added one because you keep missing your workouts."

"Why didn't she say anything to me?"

He shrugs. "Can you just drink some water and keep going? It's hot out here."

"Show me the calendar. I want to see what else that tyrant put on there."

"No."

"Why can't I see the calendar?"

"Because you're just trying to get out of swimming. I know you're tired and frustrated, but guess what, kitten, you're going to be even more tired and frustrated when your race comes and you didn't train. It's for your own good. Respect the distance."

I laugh. X smiles back. I've been trying so hard to cover up how I don't care about anything by being cheery. Even Dad noticed that I'm all smiles all the time. I even sing while I'm doing my chores. Meanwhile, I'm poring through old text messages and crying every time I can find a bathroom stall to do it in. I'm so tired I have no idea what day it is.

X, on the other hand, is exploding with energy because his semester is over. He walked at his graduation last week. Mine isn't until the end of the month. Everything will get better after that, I tell myself. It's a lot to handle, all these workouts, plus work, plus school. *You're not pathetic. It is a lot,* I say in my head.

She could do it, replies the voice inside me. The smile drops off my face. I hope X doesn't notice.

I drink some water, throw the bottle back into the kayak, and paddle out. "Ready?" X asks. I grab my goggles. As I reach for them, I spot X's phone in the clear dry bag. *Remember when that Scumbucket texted you that he loved you while he was gallivanting around Italy with his fiancée? Remember the picture of that bathtub bookstore in Venice?* my brain helpfully reminds me. What little motivation I had evaporates.

"C'mon, Mi, we'll do half. Give me one more mile. And then I've got a surprise for you."

"Is it a run? If it's a surprise run—"

"It's hiking. We're meeting everyone in . . ." He checks his watch. "In two hours, so that means we have to hustle."

"All the way out here?"

"Yeah," he says. He looks kind of . . . guilty.

For my own good, I think, treading water. I take my goggles back off.

"There's nothing on the calendar, is there. Nothing on my training plan at all. This should have been a rest day."

"What?"

He has *no* poker face. Not with me.

"You added it. *You* added the swim."

"No I didn't."

"What day is it?"

"I have no idea. Who ever knows the date, I mean really."

"It's because it's today, isn't it," I say. "His wedding is today."

X is quiet. He puts his head in his hands.

"It's happening right now, isn't it."

"Yeah," he says. My heart splits in two. I didn't know the date, but I knew it was coming. I knew it would hurt this way. *Now. Right now.*

"Give me my phone," I say as I swim to the kayak.

"Why?"

"I just want to see the pictures."

"You don't want to see that."

"Why? Because it's all beautiful on Instagram with her *perfect* #supportcrew bridesmaids taking a million *perfect* pictures of her *perfect* day?"

"No, because you're letting him ruin one more day with me. He doesn't matter, Miho. Drop it."

"Fine."

I kick away from X, treading water.

"Do you want to talk about it?" he asks.

"No," I lie. It's taking all of my self-control not to tackle the kayak and take my phone out. "Can I please get on the boat and go in?"

"No."

"I'm tired. Do you want me to drown?"

X sighs, puts the paddle in the boat.

"You're not tired—you want to get on Instagram and cyberstalk her to make yourself feel worse."

"No I don't."

"You absolutely do."

"And it's not stalking because I never said anything to her."

"It's definitely cyberstalking."

"Cyberstalking is online harassment. Look it up, you computer nerd. I have never, and will never, talk to her. Don't I get credit for that? Don't I get some kind of karmic points for not messing up her entire life when I absolutely could? When all I'd need to do is show up in her in-box with the truth?"

"I still don't know why you won't tell her."

I glare at him.

"Okay, I *do* know," he says reluctantly. "I get the logic. You know she's definitely going to have the baby, and you don't want their kid to end up . . ."

"On the side of the road alone." Tears brim in my eyes.

"Your mom didn't leave you because she thought you were worthless. She left you because she was a drug addict, and you know that," X says. "But, Miho, it's a *lie*. You're not saving their kid, because you can't change reality. He is who he is."

"People change," I say. "He did a bad thing. That doesn't mean he doesn't love her, only that he didn't love me."

"Whatever. I don't know if that's right or wrong here. I honestly don't care about either of them. It's you I care about. Whatever the masochistic cousin of cyberstalking is? That's what you're doing."

"I need to see so I can move on. I can't help it."

"You can help it. You don't want to."

"No, I can't. I try. I am trying so hard. But I can't. It's like the universe is screwing with me. Everywhere I look, there he is, or even worse, there *she* is with her perfect life. I was feeling better, and then you know what happened? I did a pizza delivery, and it was to her bachelorette party. I mean, come on. That's not fair!"

"What? When was this?"

"Like two weeks ago."

He is quiet for a moment.

"Why didn't you say anything?" he asks.

"I just didn't, okay?"

"No, it's not okay. I mean, aren't we even friends? I don't understand why you won't even talk to me."

"Because there's nothing you can do."

"I can try, Miho! Don't you think it hurts me that you won't even let me try?"

"It's not the kind of thing you understand! Do you have any idea how much it hurts to look in a mirror and just hate yourself? I hate everything about me. I don't want him back. It wouldn't fix anything. I want to turn into someone else. It hurts so, so much."

X looks like he's about to shout at me, but he doesn't.

"Of course I know what it's like to hate myself, Miho. I'm gay! At an all-boys school! On an island! With capital-C Conservative parents! You self-centered bitch! For Chrissakes, Miho. Get over it. He's just a boy. You didn't even know him that long."

"Screw you," I scream, though it's hard to flip him off when I'm treading water. "My soulmate, my partner in crime, is GETTING MARRIED at this VERY MOMENT and you want me to get over it?"

"Because he's a SCUMBUCKET and CONSTANTLY THINKING ABOUT HIM is doing NO ONE any good. And your ACTUAL FRIENDS are all trying SO HARD to make you feel better and you just want to PITY YOURSELF."

I let myself sink and get a mouthful of water so I can flip him off.

"Oh, mature."

"Give me my phone."

"No. You can wallow in wedding pictures and self-pity when you get home. Right now, you're going to finish this swim so help me god."

"Give me my phone RIGHT NOW."

"NO."

"I will flip the kayak, X, I swear."

"Go ahead. Your phone will be at the bottom of the ocean."

"SCREW YOU. SCREW YOU I HATE YOU—"

But I can't even finish the very long insult I planned.

"Go ahead and cry. You're still not getting your phone."

"I'm not crying because I want my phone. I'm crying because I'm sad. X, it's the happiest day of their lives. I mean, do you think he even thought of me once today? Even for a second?"

"I have no idea, Miho. This is too far. You have to move on. I'll do anything. Literally anything. What do I have to do to get my best friend back? What is it about him that made it so he could do this to you? I get that he was pretty and he had swoopy hair that you liked and you both liked Van Gogh and some movies and big pretentious words, but honestly, Mi? You could have that with anyone. What made you this mad for him?"

"I don't know. I really don't."

"Well, you know what sucks, Miho? What truly sucks? So many of the things that you think of belonging to Scumbucket are things we shared first. Why did you let him ruin all of those memories that are ours? Who introduced you to Nick and Nora?

Who gave you that DVD box set? Remember when *we* watched those? It hurt my feelings when you wholesale shifted that to him. And what you have in common with him has nothing on what you have in common with me. Remember when you said you'd move to San Francisco with me and be my kept woman if I became a Silicon Valley millionaire, and you'd decorate my 1920s house of sin and serve me cocktails in vintage stemware and spend all day painting and reading?"

"Yeah, I do! But we're too old for these stupid games. You're leaving me to go to college, and all of that is just make-believe, and you will never really love me."

He looks like I slapped him.

"I do really love you," he says at last. "And it hurts my feelings, Miho, that you don't think *I'm* your partner in crime."

And all of a sudden, I can see myself through X's eyes. I've been a real brat. I can see how I have been deaf to anything but the sound of my own sadness for months.

"You *are* my partner in crime," I say. "But you're not my boyfriend. And that means that someone else can break my heart. The same way all those jocks have stomped on yours. I wanted to be your everything. Every time. But even though I couldn't be, I hope I was enough."

"You were," he says. "You are."

I tread water, and the world is silent as he thinks about it. I can see him building algorithms and options in his head. But there's no system to crack, no program to build here. It's not his fault, but X does not have the answer this time.

"It can be your turn next," I say. "We can just trade off

getting dumped every year or so until we find a pair of twin amateur detectives with a large inheritance to take us away from all this."

"From your mouth to God's ears. Should we finish the swim, or do you really want to quit?"

I turn toward the shore with a sigh. God I want to go inside and watch old movies with X on the couch.

But then I look at the long stretch of ocean we've already crossed. A mile. And instead of slow, I feel strong. There's no way I could have swum that far in open water before. Maybe I'm not a bad swimmer. Maybe this is just a bad swim. I put on my goggles.

"Miho," he says. I turn back to him. "Do you think that the training is helping?"

"Real talk? Everything about this race seems completely impossible right now," I say. "Like, we still don't have a bike, I'm constantly starving, and I especially suck at running. So I think I'm screwed. Honestly."

"I meant helping with Scumbucket."

"Oh," I say. "For a second, I forgot that he's *definitely not* the reason I'm doing all this."

"So yes."

"I think so?"

"Good enough for me, partner."

chapter seventeen

"Aki-chan, knock that off," Dad calls as we climb into the pickup. "Poor Aki will never find that pink tennis ball."

Achilles abandons his dig through Mr. Kalani's flowers and comes running back to us looking as dejected as a Shiba Inu can be. It's hard to pull off being a dejected teddy bear. He tries desperately to hop up into the truck. He's too small. Dad picks him up and puts him on my lap.

"You can't bring the dog to my graduation," I tell him.

"Nonsense. I'm disabled."

I sigh. He uses that excuse for everything.

Achilles whines, licking my chin. I reach down under the seat and find a perfectly good tennis ball for him to chew on, but he just looks at it. If he can't have the pink ball, he doesn't want anything.

"It's okay, Achilles, I find it all quite meaningless as well," I say.

"It is very early for this," Dad says. "And for the last time, your diploma is not *meaningless.*"

"It's a socially constructed representation of a supposed quantity of work—"

"I appreciate that you are doing this thing you mistakenly find meaningless, but I would appreciate it more if you would spend less time theorizing about it. At least out loud."

~

The gym is about a million degrees, and we have to sit in alphabetical order, so I can't sit with my friends. We cluster together for a total of thirty seconds. We are then organized by monitors, who line us up to check in at three different stations where we collect something horrifyingly close to cattle tags that will help organize hundreds of bodies as we magically transform from "student" to "graduate." This whole thing is a joke. Even the certificate they hand us onstage is fake. I find myself being shoved around by a tidal flow of people who are all uniquely suffering this same process from individual perspectives.

My cap and gown were expensive to rent, and they are hot and I'm almost sweating through them. X isn't here. Our graduation gift to each other was not forcing each other to sit through this twice.

I arrive at my seat. It's claustrophobic being surrounded by this many people in matching gowns. If you look down the aisle at just the right angle, our knees shifting under our gowns look like the rolling ocean.

Some student gets up and talks. Our class president or valedictorian. An adult gets up, starts speaking. The boy next to me is sexting someone in this gym. His phone lights up with a picture of her crotch under one of these gross blue gowns. The girl on my other side is redoing her makeup, using her phone as a mirror, and the vibration on her phone keeps buzzing every two seconds as she gets message after message. I stare up at the rafters. At least they're not sexting each other, I guess.

Rei is the first of my crew to cross the stage, to much cheering and snaps from the student body. She's wearing bright red tights under her gown, because all the theater kids are doing that. I look at my feet. I'm wearing a plain black dress and plain black shoes. It's what we're supposed to wear. But no one gets in trouble for wearing something weird today.

I kind of wish I had worn *something* special now, though. Of course I couldn't have worn my Van Gogh sneakers even if I hadn't burned them. I still haven't been able to paint. Drawing is fine, but every time I pick up a brush, my brain wants to wander toward him. It hurts more now than when we first broke up. It's kind of like the way running hurts: a sprint hurts different than a long run. This is my marathon of heartbreak. I just have to keep going, and eventually it will end.

A cheer goes up from the crowd. It's one of the kids from the football team. We're not supposed to cheer, but football exists outside the normal rules.

In my lap, I pull up a picture of that painting. I do like it. Maybe instead of fixing my canvas, I could paint myself some new shoes.

There's a weird theory about *Wheatfield with Crows* I read once that contrasts the painful eruption of the actual way Van Gogh painted, all energy and turbulence, with what he was conveying in terms of color and subject.

That's the thing I can never get from pictures: the way he actually painted. When you see those paintings in person, you can see the way the paint stands up, the whole texture of it. I have seen exactly one Van Gogh painting in person, at the Honolulu Museum of Art. Scumbucket took me there for a date. He said it was a "simulacrum" of a real museum, because it was when he was super into using that word even when it didn't quite fit. I tried to be kind of too cool for it too, but I loved it. I was surprised that I loved the woodblock prints so much, especially the ones by this guy named Charles Bartlett. He's this English guy using a Japanese-looking technique making prints of exotic places. Scumbucket thought it was cute how into it I got, how I couldn't stop talking about the prints and kept scribbling down questions I was going to look up at the library. He called me his "little Stendhal," which was a reference to a writer he likes who had his mind blown when he went to Italy, and now has something called "Stendhal Syndrome" named after him, which is kind of like the "Double Rainbow" guy but for art. But, I don't know . . . I got the feeling that Scumbucket didn't want to talk about the prints because he didn't know anything about them, so he couldn't lecture me.

Anyway, I loved the building, and the courtyard with its pretty colored tile. It's not grand like the Rijksmuseum or the Louvre, but does everything have to be? It was beautiful in a

Hawaiian way. And when we finally got to where the one and only Van Gogh painting was, it felt so important. It's one of his wheat fields, one of those high horizon ones. I wanted to sit there for hours and sketch it. Scumbucket told me the history about it and kept pointing out facts, but in the moment, I didn't care. I wanted to *see.* In the end, he went and got a coffee while I took apart each brushstroke with my eyes. It was magic because it was real. I think, maybe, the texture is important for understanding Van Gogh. We think of images as being flat, because we usually see them on a screen or paper. But I've read that Van Gogh's work was a performance, an outpouring. You can *only* see that in the treads and tracks of his brush. So in a way, it's the artist that's lost in a print of a painting. The idea is there, but the physical act of making a painting is lost. A copy is never as good as the original.

Scumbucket would love that idea. *It's the artist that's lost in a print of a painting* is such a meaningless, pretty thought that he'd be so into. I can picture him writing it down in one of his Moleskines.

I want so badly to take out my phone and text that liar. Not anything about us. Random stuff about Van Gogh. I want to see our in-jokes volleying back and forth in alternating columns across my phone again. I want him to send me pictures of the exact page he's reading with his finger on the page because a quote made him think of me. I would give anything, literally anything, right now to see his name on the screen that—I look down and notice—seems to have navigated to my text messages.

Before my brain can intervene, my fingers pull up his number. I erased his contact, but I know his number by heart. I type in "Hey" and stop. My finger hovers above the send button.

What am I doing?

Erase it, I am telling my hands, but my fingers won't listen.

Leave it alone, I tell my hand. He is one click away in my sweaty palm. "Hey" is still ready to send beneath my hovering finger. I'm trying so hard to make myself not send that message that I'm hyperventilating.

ERASE IT. NOW.

My whole row stands up.

"Go," says the sexter.

"Huh?"

He points ahead. The row is filing out to wait closer to the stage. I look at my phone, erase the message, and shove it into my pocket. The monitor is gesturing to me wildly. I'm holding up the line. I jog toward her, holding my cap against my head. My heart is racing. My brain is in a field watching the crows. The world is silent. Before I know it, I've got an empty diploma cover in my hand, and I'm back in my seat.

~

I smile in my graduation pictures. There are lots of them. But I'm lost in my thoughts.

What is wrong with me? Why did I almost text him?

Van Gogh loved hard, like me. When he was in love with a woman who wouldn't have anything to do with him, he held his hand over a candle and begged her father to let him speak to her for as long as he could hold his hand over the flame. He needed to see her, even if it was pointless. He needed it so badly it felt like pain. I get that.

With everyone around, I don't have time to be sad. Later, Uncle Tua comes to my family's dinner and brings an ice cream cake. Dad smokes fish, which is the fanciest thing he can make outside. It comes out either blackened or burnt, depending on your outlook. After dinner, he cleans up and my neighbors try to teach me and Uncle Tua to play Go, which is really them playing by proxy.

"Not there!" Mr. Oshiro says, snatching my move away from me. He places my stone in the "correct" place. Mr. Kalani and Mr. Bu confer, then point out a move to Tua.

"Are you sure?" Tua asks. They nod in unison. Mr. Oshiro raises his eyebrows. His students are getting more clever. He has to think before we move.

"We must play with *kiai,* Miho," Mr. Oshiro says. "Not just in Go, but in life."

"What is *kiai*?"

"It is . . ." He thinks, looking for the right English word. "It is aggressiveness. It's the wind."

I put my stone down, and Mr. Oshiro shakes his head. "You let the world move you. Do not let his moves dictate yours."

"But we're playing each other. Of course his moves dictate mine," I say. Mr. Oshiro picks up my stone to change my move, but then puts it back down where I left it.

"If you are so passive, you will always lose in Go," Mr.

Oshiro says. "But that is a lesson that can only be taught by experience."

I should have listened, because we lose.

Mr. Kalani and Mr. Bu link arms and do a full end-zone dance routine, complete with imaginary football. Mr. Oshiro scolds them, but they dance even harder. Uncle Tua shrugs his shoulders. "I have no idea what just happened," he says.

"The usual nonsense. Thanks for coming," I say, and he laughs.

"It's your graduation. Of course I came. It's a big accomplishment."

"Yeah." I shrug.

"When you graduate from college, I'll do the catering, though," he says, eyeing Dad's fish suspiciously.

"If," I mutter.

"When," he says.

The party falls apart pretty early. I sit in a lawn chair watching the sky after everyone has gone.

"Training day tomorrow?" Dad asks, sitting down beside me.

"Every day," I say. "Now it ramps up, since I only have work and training."

"And college applications."

"Yeah. Eventually."

Dad is quiet for a while.

"I am so proud of you for graduating," he says. "It's a big accomplishment."

"People keep saying that. I mean, it's high school. I feel like I showed up and it just happened."

"What will ever make you feel accomplished?" he asks.

I turn back to the sky. He doesn't want to hear it.

With a great sigh, he continues: "Did I ever tell you I ran a race once?"

"No."

"It was a long time ago. Before my leg. Not anything near as ridiculous as what you are doing, or even a marathon. Just a ten-mile race. I wanted to do it with some buddies, and I wasn't sure if I'd be able to. I was macho about it. Didn't want to be embarrassed. So I trained pretty hard."

"And?"

"And what? I ran the race."

"Oh," I said. I'd been hoping it would be a better story than that.

"I shrugged it off at the time. Just a race. But much later, after the dark years"—that's what he calls the twenty years when he was an awful person, which just so happens to include me being born—"when I was recovering from my leg, I thought of it from time to time. I thought about how hard five miles had seemed when I was starting with one. I thought about how hard ten miles had seemed when I could only run five. And I think it was good, to have done it. Even if I didn't care at the time."

"There's a lesson here."

"Well, if not a lesson, a pearl of wisdom," Dad says.

Just then, something flies across the sky. Dad points to it.

"A crow!" he says. He jumps out of his seat, unusually nimble, and walks across the lawn after it.

"No," I say. "Hawaiian crows are basically extinct. There are like five, and they're all in a nature preserve, and that nature preserve is not even on this island."

"Birds fly, don't they? Maybe that was one of the five." He squints into the distance. "I think it was a lucky sign. Get your phone out in case it comes back."

"Zero percent chance."

He sits down with a sigh. "Even today, not even a bit of optimism."

"I'm just being realistic."

"You don't have to be so realistic all the time."

My turn to sigh.

"Being realistic isn't a bad thing," I say.

"It is when you won't apply to college because you're convinced it isn't realistic. You will get into any school you apply to, Miho."

I snicker.

"What's so funny?" he asks.

"You're not the only person who thinks I'll get into any school I apply to. Just not because of the SATs."

"Because of your art? I think any school would be blind not to let you in after seeing your sketches, if that's what you want to do."

I shake my head. "Not because of the art."

His eyebrows mash together as he tries to figure it out.

So I tell him about this party I went to with a bunch of kids from X's school a few years ago. About this jerk of a senior in a Vineyard Vines shirt who was *actually going* to the Art

Institute of Chicago. I was so excited to meet him. I told him I thought I'd never get in, though looking at what he called "art," I couldn't see how he did either.

"You should just apply," he said. "You're, like, Hawaiian or something? It was *really* hard for me to get in. I even got wait-listed. But minorities get into all the good schools, like automatically. You'll probably even get a sweet scholarship."

And I said, "Yeah." I even laughed a little, to show I was in on the joke.

Dad's jaw drops.

"That's *not* true," he says.

"Yeah, I know it's not true," I say. "But it's what people think."

"Well . . ." He ponders this for a second. "So what? All your friends don't care. You should stop caring too. Every single one of those kids is going to college. You are just as bright as any of them. How many of them got your score—"

"Will you *stop* with the SAT score? It's *one number.* On *one test.* It doesn't magically make all the problems with me going to college go away."

"Then why are all of your friends going to college? Why are you the only one with a problem?"

I know why. Wyatt, Trin, and X are all STEM. Lani has a business. Rei's parents can afford to float her lavish life in New York. And yes, some of my friends understand what it's like to be poor. They know how frustrating that can be. But they don't know what it's like to be scared and hungry and totally unsure if you're about to head to foster care, because one thing Hawai'i does right is *ohana.* Family. They have never been alone.

"Poor people don't get to be artists, Dad," I say.

"I looked it up. Your Van Gogh was very poor."

"He had his brother Theo."

"You have me."

"Oh yeah? And what are you going to do?" I say, meaner than I intend.

"Believe in you," he says without pausing.

I open my mouth to say something smart-alecky, but nothing comes out. Dad is my Theo, with his unshakable confidence.

But he didn't go to college. I love my dad, but I don't know if that means he's right, or can guide me here.

"Dad. I just . . . I can't. How could I ever be a painter knowing that if I ever take one wrong step, the rug gets ripped out from under me?"

"But that's true of most people, my flower. All great things require work and risk. It won't be perfect. But if it's your dream, isn't it worth trying for?"

"It's not true for everyone. Not in the same way. Think of Scumbucket, Dad. He has screwed up in ways that would completely destroy my life. But no matter what he does, he's standing on this giant pile of rugs. Some of them are even magic carpets that fly him away from all the consequences. He gets one rug pulled out from under him, and there's another, right there.

"I have *one rug,* Dad. That's why I'm *scared.* Can't you get that? I'm *scared* to apply. Because what if I *did* get in? Do I risk it? I'm not just your flower. I'm someone who has to eat and pay rent and have health insurance. And I just want to be okay, you know? I don't want to be on food stamps and I know, I *know,* there's nothing wrong with that, but I . . . I need to be okay, even if it means not being an artist. I don't want to end up like Mom. You know I love you, but I don't want to end up . . ."

I can't say it.

"You don't want to end up like me," he finishes. "I don't want you to end up like me either. That's why I want you to go to college."

"But maybe I'm supposed to stay here and work at Tua's and go to community college in a few years and paint as a hobby, you know? Isn't that a pretty okay life?"

I feel the knot of helplessness in my throat, the burning of tears in my eyes. It's not something either of us can fix. It's not something that's fair, or right, but it is true.

"I'm sorry I can't give you more rugs," Dad says after a long pause.

"I don't need you to be sorry for that. I need you to admit that it's true. I'm not lazy or chicken, you know? But it's like I'm standing on a cliff and everyone knows I can't fly, but you keep telling me to jump because maybe, *just maybe,* I'll survive. Don't you see how much that hurts, to have to kill my own dreams because you aren't willing to be realistic and kill them for me? You think I'll never be able to finish an Ironman because I can't afford a bike, so you try to protect me from it.

You think that's unrealistic? How in the world do you think I'm going to make it through college?"

Dad is quiet, and for the first time, it seems like he agrees with me. I'm right and he knows it.

The bird flies back over us. We both watch.

"I don't think that is a crow after all," he says, looking up at the sky. "No, I guess you're right. It's not a crow."

"I know," I say. "It's never really a crow."

chapter eighteen

One of the consequences of training for hours every day is that I can't go a day without it anymore. It's technically morning, the day after graduation. I switch on my PlayStation for some *Eldritch Codex,* but I know that's not what I need. I switch it off. I pace my room, and the house tilts ever so slightly under me like a boat. I'm jittery. I can't unclench my teeth.

I grab my sneakers and hop out my bedroom window.

I creep around to the side of the house and start wheeling out my bike. The moon is bright. The lawn still smells like the charcoal grill. I hop on and ride in the grass, which makes the best whirring sound, even though my feet get wet. It makes me smile every time.

My legs are a little creaky as I'm starting out, but I don't worry about it. I've learned that "warming up" is in fact not a conspiracy invented by gym teachers. In a few miles, I'm going to feel like myself. Sometimes you have to sit with the bad feeling in your body until it works itself out.

As I'm riding, it's like I'm picking apart all the knots I've tied inside myself. All the tangles start to look like string again.

I wish life were like a video game. When you start out in *Eldritch Codex,* you build your own character. Even though all the races and classes are different, everyone starts out essentially the same. You may have more strength, but that means you have less dexterity. You may have a wind affinity, but that means you have no cold resistance. No one gets to start out super powerful, and no one starts out with nothing, because then the game wouldn't be fun.

Of course, once you start playing, it's not like that at all. There's rampant gold farming, and power leveling. But as an ideal, it's not a bad one.

I finally convinced the one person who refused to see reason about college that I'm right. Everyone agrees with me now. I guess that's it. No college.

They say that people who can spot art forgeries sometimes know that the work is fake before they can say why. Tonight, that's how I feel. I can't say why this sensible life I'm setting up for myself is wrong. Yet, I know that it is.

How far do I have to bike to unravel all this?

There's a voice that speaks to me when I ride my bike forever, when the angry, sad, scared person I am most of the time can't keep up and goes quiet. Maybe that voice is the real me, the one no one else knows.

As the sun comes up, I see where my bike-brain took me.

It's the field. The last dairy farm on Oahu. The one where I painted my copy of Van Gogh. The cows are all standing around near the fence, and beyond it, it's a green field. My wheat field, with no wheat.

In this moment, breathless, my heart pounding, I'm okay. Maybe the reason I tried to text Scumbucket at my graduation is because I didn't go running before the ceremony. Maybe that tidal wave of sadness and panic was a product of my chemical addiction to endorphins. A lie my hormones are telling me.

There's nothing more I can get from him. The things I want, they're not lost in the past with him. They're somewhere out there in the future, at my finish line. All I have to do is figure out how to get there. Maybe everything until now was the warm-up, and now I'm finally ready to do the hard work of letting him go.

The truth: I *want* to go to college. It's what I've always wanted. It broke my heart when I let the deadline for applications pass. But I couldn't do it.

Because what if I fail?

Now I can finally see the other side: What if I live my life knowing I never even tried?

Dad is my Theo. And so are my uncles, Tua, my friends. All those people are my *ohana* of Theos.

And even if Dad can't help me, he'll try. Maybe I won't even need help. I got that 1600 all on my own, just me and a book from the library, working practice test sets night after night, month after month. Not even X knows how hard I worked for that score.

I'm just so tired of working so hard even to get to the starting line. But one thing I know now, after all the work I've put in so far on this race, is that I have endurance on my side. And it's not a personality trait, it's a skill. One I've practiced.

I know what I have to do.

I stop at the library on my way home. I go to one of the terminals. I go to the website I have memorized. I print out the Common Application (at least, the first twenty pages, which is what's free per day), and when I pick the pages up, they are warm and nice to hold.

I like seeing this application as a real thing, not pixels on a screen. I like holding this stack of papers in my hands.

At home, I tape the first page up next to my training plan.

I glance at the plan. Tomorrow's workout: easy thirteen-mile run.

I love the double meaning of *run*. You can run the world by being in charge, or you can run the world by going from place to place. I don't want to run the world like Beyoncé means it. I want to run the world by being in it. More girls should get to run the world.

Running seemed impossible a few months ago. That's the way you start anything: with a single step.

chapter nineteen

It is two weeks later, in Trinity's garage. Her brothers are inside the house, and you can hear the weight of four grown men moving around. The light hanging from the garage ceiling swings, and I understand why she spends so much time out here. Her house is bursting.

Trinity lifts up her welding mask. "Science can only do so much."

My bike lies on her workbench. She unzips the long front zipper of her dark gray jumpsuit and slips off the arms, steps out of the legs with her shoes still on. Underneath, she's wearing her favorite galaxy-print swimsuit.

"Were you swimming?" I ask.

"I have more swimsuits than underwear," she says. Then she breaks into a grin. "Ever since I got my acceptance, I've been getting up early to swim. You know how hard it is to do a spacewalk?"

"Very?"

"Not quite an Ironman, but it's all in the arms."

Trinity raises the garage door and lets in some real light. While she's putting things away, I look at my phone. A message from Rei.

"Where are you?" Rei asks, just to me, off the group chat.

"Trin's. Want to come hang?"

"Are you with Wyatt?"

"No. Why? Is he meeting us?"

"Can't get ahold of him. Nvm."

"Who's that?" Trin asks.

"Rei," I say. "Looking for Wyatt."

Trin snorts.

"What?"

"Trying to catch Wyatt, more like," she says.

"What do you mean?"

"Catch him cheating," Trinity says. I incline my head. "She thinks he's cheating. It's so obvious."

I shake my head. "He wouldn't do that."

"Yeah," Trinity says. "But Rei's like super jealous. Sometimes I wonder if she has too much money and time on her hands."

"She's just in love," I say.

"Probably," Trinity says. "Broke people get jealous too. Anyway."

All around us, her mad-scientist lab tools hang in chaotic disarray on pegboards. She has enough machinery here to build rockets, *which she has done.* (And gotten us both grounded for. Apparently, rockets can light things on fire if some idiot miscalculates their trajectory.) This stuff is all junk compared to what's in her room: her prize telescope, worth more than her oldest brother's car, and all its accessories. She has it bike-locked to her bed *in her own house.* She won it in a contest that was supposed to spread good will for the telescopes on Mauna Kea. She wrote about how strongly she felt about respecting her Hawaiian heritage, and being a future astronaut. She never did let me read it, but whatever she concluded, she won. What my bike is to me, Trin's telescope is to her. I would not let anyone I didn't trust with my life touch this bike. I don't care if it's a piece of garbage. It's the most important thing I own.

Trin glares down at my bike, shaking her head. "I hate to break it to you, but you are basically riding a cow catcher. It's way too heavy, and your handlebar position means you can't get into a maximally aero position. It's way too big for you. And what is this disaster here? Did you weld this?"

"Mr. Bu welded it. After Dad ran it over with the car."

"And this is what we've got to work with," Trin says, trying to see past my bike's history written in raised metallic scars and scratches. I know she's trying to see its potential, trying to love it like I do so she can see what it *could be* instead of what it *is.*

Trinity sighs. "No, I'm sorry. It's not about how it looks, it's about what it can do. Can you even lift it?"

I grab the frame, pick it up, and try to hoist it over my head like cyclists do on Instagram. I do, but my arms are shaking. Trin grins.

"Yeah, hold that for a minute," she says. "I'll time you."

"I would prefer not to," I say with a groan as I let it down again. "I read that lightweight bikes are overrated anyway, and it's all about wind resistance."

"Woo, someone's been googling," Trin says. "That's true. To a point. But there are other factors. I mean, from an engineering standpoint, it looks like someone repurposed trash into a bike."

"Bricolage," I say.

"Huh?"

"*Bricolage* is when you make do with what you have and turn it into what you need."

Trin sneers. "Is that from a Scumbucket book?"

"No. It's an art term," I say. I can't remember if I told Scumbucket about it, or if he told me. But either way, it's my word now. I happen to like it.

"Bricolage," she tries out. She smiles, nods. "Well, as impressive as this *bricolaged* bike is, I don't know what I can do with this. I could grab some pipes and build a new one from scratch and we'd come up even."

"You could not."

"Totally could," she says.

"So what do we do?"

"We need to get you a new bike. A real bike, if possible."

"Trin, we have three hundred dollars budgeted for the bike. There *is* a real bike under here, I swear."

"Maybe we can rent a super bike," Trinity says. "I can MacGyver almost anything we need, but I can't manifest you a carbon frame." She looks around at her equipment and throws up her hands.

"So what's the plan?"

"Keep working with what we have, and hope for a miracle."

"Anything is—"

"Let's not jinx it."

Trinity and I ride over to the bike store for the easy stuff we need with her on my pegs. It's hard to go fast with someone standing over your back tire, but I like the challenge. Plus I'm biking for my bike's honor. I can't let Trin see how hard this is.

"How do you normally get around?" I ask her between panting breaths.

"Magic," she replies.

"But how really? Do you text someone? Call someone? It's like you get beamed up places. Like *Star Trek.* I don't think any of us have seen you pull up in a car."

"Every girl's got her secrets."

"I bet you're driving a pink Cadillac convertible and your parents are millionaires."

She doesn't laugh, which is weird. Her hands tense on my shoulders.

"What would you buy with a million dollars?" she asks.

"I don't know," I say. It's a question I think about a lot, though. What I would do if I were rich. "You?"

"Freedom," she says.

"You can't buy freedom," I say.

"But you can put freedom in a bank," she says. "You can put a million dollars in a bank and then say, well, no matter what happens, I'll be okay."

"Do you honestly think it works that way, though?"

"Yes."

"Trinity, what's up?"

She sighs.

"Nothing. I'm just worried about college."

"You're not paying for it, though. Financial aid."

"Yeah, but I still have to live."

"You got room and board. You got a free ride. You'll be fine."

"Do you think so? I don't know. I mean, yeah, I'll have enough money to eat and study. Even my textbooks are paid for. But do you know how much a plane ticket from Boston to Hawai'i is?"

I shake my head.

"It's a lot. It's a *lot* a lot around the holidays."

"Are you worried that you'll miss your family?"

"Yeah. My family, and . . . other things. Is that why you didn't apply for college?"

"No," I say. "I just . . . didn't. I'm going to. I needed time to wrap my head around it."

"I get that," she says. "I kind of wish I'd wrapped my head around it before I had to do it."

We ride in silence. The uneven sound of my feet pushing the pedals is bad form, I know, but going up a hill with Trinity on the back, I can barely move the bike even on my lowest gear. I stand to get more leverage. Trinity is right. This is almost impossible.

"It's only four years," I say at last, though I know that doesn't make it any better.

"But I keep thinking if I had a million dollars, I could go to college and not feel like I'm a) representing the entirety of my lineage as a sainted first-generation college student and b) marooned halfway across the world from everything I know and love. Like, do they have shave ice in Boston? I've never been homesick. I've never been away from home."

"I mean, it's Boston, not Mars. I knew what *poke* was before I came to Hawai'i."

"But it's not the same."

"I know."

And all of a sudden, it hits me: after this summer, after my race, we're all going our separate ways.

It'll never be the same.

"I guess that's what social media is for," Trinity says at last. "Will you get Instagram so we don't lose each other?"

"We won't lose each other even without Instagram," I say. "Besides, Instagram is for showing off your perfect life. My life isn't ever going to be Instagrammable."

"Mine is. Everyone likes pictures of E. coli in zero G conditions right?"

"Uh, no."

"How about artsy black-and-white posts of article citations with fifteen authors, where I'm the fourteenth author?"

"That'll get some likes."

"It'd get one more if you would get Instagram. Put pictures of Achilles up. He's an internet gold mine. Everyone loves a tripod dog."

"I'll agree to lurk once you're in your dorm."

"I'm holding you to that."

We pull up to the bike store, and I want to say how everything will be okay and she's going on to this brilliant future and how much I admire her and how awesome I think she is and all this other stuff. But instead, she gets off the bike, we look at each other, and she does the most Trinity thing ever. She punches me in the shoulder.

"What was that for? I just biked you across half this island!" I say, punching her back and missing.

"Don't leave an opening next time."

"Thanks, Cato."

"Who is Cato?"

"Have you never seen *The Pink Panther*?"

"Is it some stupid X movie?"

I'm going to tell her, but she swipes at me again. My fists are up, and I have no idea why we're boxing, but we are, because that's what Trin does when things get emotional. Given how much we wrestle, I am starting to think Trinity isn't as hard as she seems. She gets me in a choke hold and I'm about to tap out, but then we hear a door open and a guy wearing a half apron and a bright yellow T-shirt that says "Tour de France" on the front is staring down at us.

Before he can say anything, Trinity lets me go.

"Kyle?" she asks.

"Yeah," he says. "What are you—"

"Cross-training. Don't you box? It keeps the athlete nimble," Trinity says, slapping me hard on the back.

"The athlete?" he asks.

"The athlete," she says, pointing to me. "Gotta keep her on her toes. Anyway, I called earlier about time trial bikes?"

"You?"

Trinity has turned off her accent, because this guy doesn't have one, but even speaking right does you limited good when someone has moments ago watched you brawling in the street.

"We're mostly interested in looking today, and purchasing a few smaller items, but I had some questions about bike fitting and possible upgrades on an existing frame," Trinity says, pushing her hair back and staring him down. He looks at her hard. Then his eyes move to me. Finally, he spots my bike lying in the dirt and recoils.

"That's not the frame, is it?"

"We're working with a generous definition of the word 'possible' these days," Trinity says. "Let's talk shop."

~

"Girls, I don't know what to tell you," Kyle says, running his hand over my bike. "There's not much we can do for this bike to get you closer to what you want."

"It's what I expected," Trinity says. "And you're saying we could get a new one for . . ."

"In your price range, there's not a lot. There's basically nothing. Is three hundred dollars the absolute highest you can go?"

Trinity and I look at each other, then back at him. We nod.

Kyle isn't fazed. Once he got over the shock of us, he got super into finding me a bike. Thank god for nerds. Getting a bike fitted is like hundreds of dollars, but Kyle was bored and we were amusing, so he spent most of the afternoon explaining it to us and letting us try out stuff in the completely dead store. When I tried to stop wasting his time, he kept coming up with new toys for us to play with, including some bikes I could never afford but definitely wanted to ride around the block. There's a big flat stretch outside, and Kyle let me take a Corneille road bike out of the shop. I guess he thought I wouldn't leave Trin to take the fall if I decided to steal it? But I might love this bike more than I love Trinity. Not really. I think.

"Okay, well, let's dream a little," he says. "Do you want a tri bike?"

Trin and I shake our heads.

"I still have to ride it everywhere," I say. "I can't deliver pizzas on a Cervélo P5."

"Understood," he says. "So we want versatile."

"We want Corneille. We'll settle for anything better than my frankenbike."

He looks over his shoulder at a poster hanging on the corkboard. He takes it down. "You know, though, there's this local triathlon club that's giving away a Corneille tri bike with all these sweet integrated components—"

"I don't need charity," I say.

"I beg to differ," Trinity says.

"It's a contest," Kyle says. "These ladies are cool. I know their president, Aaliyah. She'd love this race you guys are doing. You might win it, with your great story. Look, this is the third year they've run it. This girl won last year, and now she's on a college tri team in Arizona. Got a scholarship and everything."

He points to a picture hanging on the wall. A girl a little older than me is standing with a beautiful Corneille triathlon bike, smiling like she's trying to break her face. Judging by the matching uniforms, I'm guessing it's the Pipeline Tri Club gathered around her. They're so different than the triathletes I saw on TV. First and foremost, they're all women. And some of them have curly hair or braids or even shaved heads, and some of them are athletic and some are fat and some have big biker thighs, and they all have different skin colors. They look like normal people. Awesome people.

Maybe I should enter. I would give anything for that bike.

But when I look at the picture again, I notice that the girl with the bike is also holding a sign. It says SECOND ANNUAL RECIPIENT OF THE CORNEILLE CHARITY TRIATHLON BIKE. *Charity. Recipient.* Not *contest winner.* I can practically see myself in that picture, saying, "I never would have gotten here without the kind charity of others. I am so grateful for the opportunities I have been given, and will do my best to live up to the gifts I have received." But I want to say, "I am so proud of this thing I did all on my own, because I'm awesome."

Charity erases all the work you put in.

My race is not a gift. It's something I am working harder on than anything I've ever done.

If I take this charity bike, that will ruin it.

I want to earn the things I have.

"I'd rather work with what we can afford," I say.

"Okay," Kyle says, putting the poster back up. I'm so grateful he doesn't make a big deal out of it. Trinity looks at me and nods. She may not like it, but she gets it.

"So we want a Corneille road bike that costs three hundred dollars. That's not going to happen. So how can we get close?"

"Could we rent a bike for a single day?"

"Our store doesn't do that, and I'd recommend against it. You need something you can train on." He turns to me. "*Never* debut your gear in a race setting. Never."

"Well, we're screwed," Trinity says.

"Tell you what. Give me your email and I'll ask around about used bikes. I can't promise anything. But, I mean, literally anything would be better than this."

"Gee, thanks," I say.

"Miho, it's an awesome bike. It's *your* awesome bike. But you don't bring a knife to a gunfight, no matter how kickass your knife is."

"I don't think we're going to have a choice," Trinity says. "Thanks for everything, Kyle. Like, you're the man. Or the gender-neutral entity of your choice."

"Man's fine. I do have a few treats I can help you out with here in the store." He looks at me. "*Not* charity. Damaged stuff I can give you with a steep discount and samples."

"We can pay."

"It's not charity between friends," he insists.

He retreats behind the counter and into a back room and returns with an armful of open boxes and bags a few minutes later.

"So already we got you the pedals, and the cleats, and we got you the shoes off the sale rack. Sorry about the color," Kyle says, pointing to the stuff Trinity's got in her shopping bag. The shoes are a sunny, golden yellow. There's a reason they were on the sale shelf. I kind of like them, though. They remind me of my Van Gogh sneakers. My face falls as I remember them on fire in that oil drum. I remember how—

"Miho, check this out. This is gonna be sweet," Trinity says. I peer at what she's holding in her hand. It's a silver cartridge, kind of like a tiny blimp.

"Whippets?" I ask.

"CO2," Kyle says. "I hope kids don't do whippets anymore. You're shooting holes in your brain."

"So what is it?" I ask.

"You can use it to change a tire lightning-quick without a pump," Trinity says.

"You wanna try it?" he asks Trinity.

"Absolutely. Time me, bike man."

~

We leave the store with a giant shopping bag full of open store samples, lightly scuffed gear, and Kyle's phone number for bike questions. All at the low, low price of my last paycheck, which is all we had for accessories. The stuff we're carrying is worth about three times that.

When we get into Trinity's garage, she hoists my bike onto her table again.

"I think I could do it on my own bike. It would just be slow," I say.

"I know," Trinity says. "But we wanted this race to be as real as possible. We're going to time you and everything. And I don't want the bike to be the reason you were slower than you could have been. I want to make sure I did everything I could."

"Even if the bike falls apart, it wouldn't be your fault."

"When I'm in space, I want to know that all the work that went into me getting there was the best work possible, not only because it makes me faster, but because of what it means for the world, and for science and . . . stuff. Like, if I build a rocket to send someone into space, I want to be proud of it. If I am on a rocket, I want it to be something someone is proud of. Our best work makes us better. Our best work makes *the world* better."

"Lame."

"So lame. Such nerd."

"Look, I know you want me to have a great bike, but don't let it get you down."

Trinity has put her jumpsuit back on. She grabs one of her fire-spewing torch things and hands me a mask and fireproof jacket.

"You know what JFK said about trying to get to the moon?" she asks.

"No, what?"

"He said we do these things 'not because they are easy, but because they are hard.' Everything that makes you *you* goes into the hardest things you meet head-on: your humor, your creativity, your whole heart. That's why I think, as JFK put it, 'we choose to go to the moon.' "

She says that last line in a weird voice, and it takes me a second to realize she's doing her best JFK impersonation. I laugh.

"Trinity, if anyone will be an astronaut, it's you."

"But even if I never am one, I couldn't go my whole life and not try. Yeah, reality is reality. But, this is the effort that *organizes me,* you know? Like, as a person," she says. "It's what I have to do. And maybe in our lifetime we'll go to Mars. Maybe I'll walk on another planet. Maybe I'll fix one piece of shielding on one satellite no one but space nerds cares about, and right then I'll know that every sacrifice I made was worth it, just to be the person whose best was brought out by getting someone else there. I have to try, Miho. It's pointless to be sad because I know there's no other choice for me. I wish it didn't feel like such a risk."

Maybe I'm not the only person in my crew who is scared.

"Nothing is ever certain," I say. "For anyone."

"I know," she replies. "But for some more than others."

"I get it. You feel like you're standing on one rug, and you know if it gets ripped out from under you, there's nowhere to go but down."

"Yeah," Trinity says.

"You can always come hang out on my rug, for what it's worth. Or Lani's. Or X's. Or Rei's. Or Wyatt's."

Trinity smiles. She flips down the front of her welding mask. Heart-to-heart over.

"Are you sure about this?" She leans over my bike like a surgeon.

"Unequivocally," I say. "I choose to go to the moon."

chapter twenty

X and I go to his house after my four-and-a-half-hour bike ride on my imperfect but very tricked-out bike. We sit in his room and binge-watch *The Avengers.* His mom and dad make us keep the door open, but they also make his brothers vacate their own bedroom, so it's kind of half-and-half on the trust thing.

It's a sleepy afternoon, and I fade in and out of the show. I'm more tired than I expected after my morning ride. I must have been going harder than I thought. Trinity did wonders. I can tell how much of a difference it makes, these little changes. An angle. A few ounces. Even if it can't be perfect, it makes a difference. I can tell how much more powerful I am with my yellow bike shoes and new clip-in pedals. And the best part: she made the pizza rack removable with one hex key instead of a whole toolbox. #aero #stillemployed

I biked almost a hundred miles today, harder and farther than I thought was possible, on legs exhausted from the day before. Not to mention the day before that, and the day before that. I feel awesome.

"You watching, or are you sleeping?" X asks as he switches to the next DVD.

"Watching," I say, even though the last thing I remember was the opening credits.

"I know you were sleeping."

"Was it the snoring or closed eyes that gave it away?"

"You slept through like half this season."

"I have never been this tired in my entire life."

"It's still not too late to drop out," X says. "Instead of all this work, we could phone in the rest of the summer on the couch. *The Avengers* was on forever."

"Why would I want to do that? I did awesome today."

"Because tomorrow's your long run."

I groan until I literally run out of breath and have to gasp and start groaning all over again.

"How long is long?" I whine.

"Twenty-one miles. Easy pace."

"I'm pretty sure 'twenty-one-mile easy run' is an oxymoron."

"So quit."

"Why are you trying to get me to quit after we've put in so much work? Do you think I'm not working hard enough?"

"I'm not, and you are," X says, wrapping his arms around me. "Sometimes I miss . . . us. The people we used to be."

"Me too."

"Like, it's great that we hang out and do sports stuff all the time. But is this who we are now?"

"We're all of it. You know what? Next rest day, we should go to your birthday restaurant. For no reason. We can dress up fancy."

"Really?"

"Or whatever you want to do," I offer. "Anything you want."

"I want—"

"*Except* break into the Disney resort." We used to do that all the time when we were younger. You need a special wristband to get into the pool, but if you're small, it's not difficult to sneak around.

He rolls his eyes. "I wasn't going to suggest that."

"You totally were."

"Fine. I totally was. Okay, restaurant."

"Do you mind the sports stuff?" I ask.

"No." He shakes his head. "Just missing you. I hope this is what you need."

"Right now, the only thing I need is John Steed," I reply.

~

X's mom feeds us the good red ramen with eggs for dinner. We leave my bike at his place. I can barely walk. He waits until I make it to my front steps before leaving. He waves at me as he pulls away. I blow him a kiss.

"He's a good friend," Dad says behind me, watching through the screen door.

"He's the *best* friend," I say, still watching the taillights. He rode Lani's scooter next to me for four and a half hours today. He almost had to carry me to the car once the soreness set in, and he'll be back tomorrow with a smile on his face.

"How do his parents not know he's gay?" Dad asks.

"Good old-fashioned denial."

"Well, it'll be nice that he'll be around next year," Dad says.

"But then he'll be gone too."

"Nowhere you couldn't follow," Dad says. "But I understand. You have to 'do you,' as the kids say." He puts a hand on my shoulder, and then he goes back into the house.

It's true, I think, trying to will my legs to stand me up. Maybe I could follow X to Cornell. It'd be a stretch, but maybe I could.

I haven't even told Dad about applying to college yet. I think some dreams are better as a secret, especially when they're scary. But without Dad constantly pressuring me to apply—now that I know it's *really* my choice—it's been so easy. Fill out a form. Ask for a recommendation. Write an essay. Get a transcript. Everything is one step in front of another. Applications don't even open until August, and I have until mid-November to finish, to make it totally perfect. I'm ready.

I don't know where I'm headed. But I know it's not Cornell, not to follow my best friend.

I'll miss him, though.

"Stand up," I tell myself out loud, and I do.

In my room, it's all I can do to peel my clothes off. My legs are hot. It's like they're generating heat even though my ride ended hours ago. I don't even want the water in the shower hot because I'm boiling inside.

I'd like to stay in the shower forever, but tomorrow is coming. I get out and go to my room. I can't, I think. Twenty-one miles. I can't face it. I can't do it. My legs are done.

Something makes me remember, and I pull open my dresser, digging through it until I find it.

I get dressed. And then I am dead out.

~

"Up," X says, and I curse the time travel that brought me to this moment with no apparent sleep in between.

I pull the covers over my face.

The covers vanish, and my whole body snaps into a fetal position.

"Aren't we fancy," X says.

"Rei," I explain. I am a knot of racing stripes. Matchy-matchy.

"Are you wearing your running shoes in bed?" X asks.

"Motivation."

"For the record, you wanted this."

I feel something cold wedge its way into my clenched hands.

"Get out of bed and drink the smoothie, partner. We're already late."

I slide out of bed and onto the floor. The smoothie is good.

"I like the outfit," he says.

"Rei called it my power costume. She said it would make me feel like a superhero."

"Do you?"

"No."

"It's probably the bedhead."

X sits behind me on the bed, undoing the knot I was hoping looked something like a French braid. He brushes my hair and I get that weirdly pleasant skritchy sensation of someone else doing your hair. I integrate more smoothie into myself. I become slightly more human.

A headband wraps itself over my braided pigtails, which I don't even have to look at to know are now perfect.

"You'd be a more convincing drill sergeant if you weren't so goddamn gay all the time," I say.

"You clearly know nothing about the military."

He pushes me, and this time I manage to get off the floor and onto my feet. I glance at myself in the mirror. I look like one of those Lululemon ads. No. I look like a triathlete. Battle braids, like Lucy Charles-Barclay. It's weird, but I do feel lighter. Almost like I can fly.

Another blip in time, and I'm in the parking lot on the longest stretch of sidewalk we could find. I try to imagine the Aloha Tower behind me, like at the first Ironman.

"I think I can, I think I can," I whisper.

"What are you muttering to yourself?" X asks as he gets his bike out.

"I'm trying to get all the bad words out of my system," I say.

I do some of the stretch things Rei emphasized that I must do. Foot to butt, crossed-legs toe touching, superhero lunge.

"Ready?" asks X as he climbs onto his bike. And, surprisingly, I am.

~

Twenty-one miles. I am at mile eighteen. Pain is a sense I left back at thirteen. At fifteen, I lost the feeling in my right foot. My legs keep shuffling. Just keep going, I tell myself. I stare straight ahead.

X is riding next to me, going so slow the bike wobbles. He keeps asking if I want water. It feels like every thirty seconds, but I can't think. I hear him, but I don't respond. It's hot. So hot.

One step at a time, I tell myself. One step at a time. But my legs won't lift. I look down and I can see that I'm still running, but I can't feel it. I'm scared, then I'm elated, then I'm confused. But I can't stop. Can't stop. Stop. Can't stop. Something in my calf is seizing and it feels like I'm wearing cement boots. I think I'm crying. I can't even tell because I'm covered in sweat. My fingers feel huge.

I fall to my knees. I think I skinned my knee. I stand again and keep running.

X is off the bike. He's saying I need to stop. I think he's shouting. But it's only three more goddamn miles. He's saying something again, but I ignore him and keep going.

The pavement shimmers golden. I see the air, rustling through the fields that aren't there. Birds lift off, and for one moment the whole of it is still, the birds catching the force under their wings, letting it sweep them wherever they wish. Flying isn't fighting. It's letting the wind move you.

I hear X saying something, but the thing I feel is my palms hitting the ground. Then I'm lying there, and then I'm gone.

chapter twenty-one

X watches me nervously as I eat some onigiri he got from the 7-Eleven and drink two full bottles of Gatorade like I've been in a desert. "It's not on the nutrition plan," I insist, but he makes me eat them anyway. *Some* onigiri becomes *many* as X makes trip after trip back inside for more. I am so hungry I barely get the plastic wrap off before shoving them in my mouth. I have grains of rice sticking to my hair.

I ride on the back of his bike to meet up with our crew. I hurt so much. At this point, I'm used to being in constant pain. I walk around with the uncertainty of a fawn, on legs that no longer respond the way I'm expecting. I have tired muscles that mock me when I give them commands. They do what I tell them. Just not right away, and not always right.

We meet up on the beach, and it takes all my effort to get off the bike. My stomach is cramped. I am so nauseous I never want to move again. X is looking at me with genuine concern.

"I'm fine," I tell him. I need to put a brave face on this, not for me, but for X.

"I swear this is the last time I'm going to ask, but I'm scared. Think about it. Do you want to stop?" he asks.

"Stop what?"

"Training. The race."

I cut him off before the others can hear.

"No," I say firmly. "Absolutely not."

"No one will blame you if you want to stop. We'll say your dad said you're not allowed."

"I can't stop."

"Why? This is killing you."

"Because . . ."

"Can you please try to explain it to me?"

"I need to do this. I need to know that I can."

"I hate that he did this to you. You never needed to know these things before."

"It isn't him," I say. "I need to know it for me."

"And what do you even care what he thought about you? He was such a poser."

"I don't," I say, which is mostly true. "X. It's not about that anymore. It's bigger than that."

X sighs. "I know."

"Sounds like you were bonking," Rei says when she hears about my misadventure. "And then you kept going. Which is bad."

"Bonking?" I ask.

"She was bonking in public?" Trinity asks.

". . . yes?" Rei says hesitantly.

"Miho, that's gross."

"What exactly do you think *bonking* means, Trinity?" Rei asks.

"It sounds like a sex thing."

"Not everything is a sex thing."

"I'm pretty sure *bonking* means doing it."

"No, it's a running term—"

But Trinity's already got her phone out, and is showing us her findings. "Internet says doing it."

"Let me see that," Rei says. She looks at the phone and rolls her eyes.

"Fine. It's also called 'hitting the wall,' " Rei says.

"That *could* be a sex thing," Trinity says.

"It's not a sex thing! Will you let me finish?"

"That's what she said."

We are all laughing, and the laughing hurts so much I can't breathe. My insides are in pain. I'm a little worried about that. I hope it's muscle pain and not some kind of organ failure.

I look over and I notice that Lani is laughing, but she's looking at Trinity. Like, really looking. She catches me watching and turns away.

"Whatever you call it, it's a nutrition problem," Lani says. "What did you eat?"

"Whatever you wrote down for me to eat this morning."

"But, like, were you hungry? Were you tired? What did you eat while you were running?"

"Who eats while they're running?"

"People who are running twenty-one miles," Rei says. "Pretty sure I told you that."

"Yeah, I ate all that before I ran so I wouldn't have to stop," I say. Lani brings her hand to her forehead, and Rei shakes her head.

"Doesn't work like that," Rei says.

"It saves time."

"Nope. Doesn't work like that. So that's problem one."

"Were you hungry?" Lani asks.

"I mean, I was starving. I've been starving this whole time."

"What?"

"I'm always starving," I say.

"You shouldn't be starving," Lani says.

"I'm sorry," I say.

"No, I don't mean you shouldn't, like, you're not allowed to be starving. I mean shouldn't, like, if you're starving, there's something obviously wrong."

She looks at the menu she wrote out. "Why didn't you say anything?"

"Because you told me what to eat and I ate it!"

"But if it wasn't right for you, why wouldn't you say something?"

"You know so much about food. I assumed I wasn't trying hard enough. I thought that the problem must be me."

"And that's what trashes female athletes," Rei says. She takes me by the shoulders. "Starving. Athletes. Do. Not. Perform. Well. Period." She emphasizes each word by shaking me, and I'm too proud to tell her it hurts.

Oh, I realize. Pride. That's part of the problem.

"Food isn't a one-size-fits-all thing. That's why you need to tell someone if you, say, are feeling constantly woozy and vaguely psychotic because you're hungry. There's no universal formula. There are guidelines, but there are so many variables, and what works for one person won't necessarily work for another."

Lani thinks for a minute.

"I've got an idea," she says, gathering up her bag. "Let me see what I can do."

~

A week later, we stand in a line, waiting for the signal. My heart is pounding.

"Ready?" Lani asks. The rest of us nod. "Three . . ."

How bad will it be?

"Two . . ."

I can't. I can't.

"One . . ."

Okay. Head in the game.

"Go!"

We each rip the top off homemade foil packets and pop squares of goo somewhere between the texture of a gummy bear and glue into our mouths. They've got liquid-y centers.

"Not bad!" Rei says with relief.

"It's salty because of electrolytes," Lani says.

"Mr. Oshiro says electrolytes are government propaganda to get you to buy expensive sports drinks," I say, struggling to chew.

"Nope," she replies. "Not true."

"It's good," I say. "Kind of not sure I can chew this while running."

"I'll work on it."

We are in Trinity's garage, the evidence of this project all around us. I'm slightly concerned that Trinity's science experiments may have taken place on this same table, given that she went through a bacteria-obsessed phase, but Lani's a pro. We probably won't die.

"How many calories are in this?" Rei asks.

"Fifty a square."

"So they're like the least healthy candy on the planet. What is the difference between this and a handful of jelly beans?"

"Electrolytes, complex carbs, caffeine, and some Miho-specific science-ing courtesy of Trinity's Littlest Chemist set."

"What is this flavor? I can't place it," X says. I watch as he discreetly spits his into a handkerchief that of course he is carrying. He raises a finger to his lips when he catches me watching.

"We went with POG. Everyone loves POG," Trinity says.

"I still think POG is an elaborate joke you guys are playing on me," I say.

"California Niece," Trin says, shaking her head.

"Well, even if POG isn't a thing—"

"It *is* a thing!"

"—I still dig it. These are great, Lani."

"So you eat these *during* the long run and long bike, not *before,*" Rei says.

"During," I confirm.

"Another?" Lani asks. "These ones are pineapple."

"Gimme!" I say. She tosses one to me. I take a step forward, trying to catch it, and my left leg buckles. I hear Lani gasp. I see X reach out to catch me, but Wyatt springs forward, knocking into Rei. I catch myself before I hit the ground, and then Wyatt and I are standing there face-to-face, and Rei is picking herself up off the floor.

"Priorities, darling," she says, looking at us, dusting herself off.

"I'm so sorry," I say, going to Rei. I put a hand on her shoulder. "Are you okay?"

She shoves my hand off.

"No, no. I see how it is," she says. "How's that game you guys like? Or is it pictures back and forth? Good old-fashioned sexting?"

Wyatt sighs. "Rei, you're being ridiculous."

"Am I, though? Or am I just not being a sucker."

Wyatt throws up his hands. It's so horrifyingly awkward that I want to disappear. Lani and Trin obviously feel the same way, because they are silent as mice slinking into the shadows.

"I want to talk to you," Wyatt says. "Can we go?"

"No. Say what you have to say," Rei says. Wyatt looks around nervously.

"Fine. You've been acting jealous for weeks now, trying to see what's on my phone. If you can't trust me, then we shouldn't be dating."

"So show me what's on your phone and I won't be jealous," Rei says. She holds out her hand.

"Rei, there's *nothing* on my phone."

"Then why can't I see it?"

"Because it's *private.*"

"Wait," I say, finally catching up. "You think Wyatt and I have been texting behind your back?"

Rei turns to me, scowling. "Oh, I didn't want to think that. But, I mean, what was that?"

"I fell. He was being a Boy Scout, like he *always is,*" I say.

"He *pushed me out of the way to get to you,*" she says.

"Rei," I say, but then I shake my head. After what happened to me with Scumbucket, nothing is going to make her feel better but incontrovertible proof. I dig my phone out of my pocket. I unlock it. I hold it out to her. "Here. Read all my text messages. I don't care."

"Rei, if you touch that phone, I swear to god I'm breaking up with you," Wyatt says. Rei scowls at him, but she doesn't take the phone.

"Fine. You basically confirmed it anyway."

"No he didn't!" I shout. I scroll to the only messages between me and Wyatt off our group chat. They're all about swimming drills and asking him about training numbers and stupid homework questions back when school was in session. And, as I'm looking, some memes. And a few pictures of Achilles, and of his cat. His Boy Scout badges above his bed. And a few inside jokes. Wow, Wyatt and I have been talking a lot.

But it's not like we were cheating! That would literally have never occurred to me!

I hold my phone out again for Rei, but she's watching Wyatt walk out of the garage.

"You know what? You're not breaking up with me, I'm breaking up with you!" Rei shouts after him.

"No, don't go," I say.

"Stay out of this," Rei says, but I'm already chasing after Wyatt.

"Wyatt, please," I say, but he's still walking, already on the sidewalk. I grab his hand. "Hold up."

"Miho, I'm sorry," he says. He gives me a hug. "Good luck."

"But we're friends," I say, his arms still wrapped around me.

"Of course we are," Wyatt says. "I'm not friend-breaking up with you, if you don't want me to. I just thought, you know, because of Rei . . ."

"Rei will get over it. I wish you guys could work it out, and I hope you get back together, but you don't have to go because of her. No one thinks of you as *just* Rei's boyfriend. You're our friend, Wyatt. For real. You should stay." He hugs me tighter.

"Thanks, Mi," he says.

"Seriously?" Rei says behind me. I think she heard me. Wyatt releases me. Everyone else is in the garage staring. "You 'don't think of him as my boyfriend'?"

"I said he's *our* friend. Not *just* your boyfriend. Because he's a person, not an accessory, and I like hanging out with him."

"I bet you do."

"Rei!" Wyatt tries to interject.

"You're so mystified by Scumbucket two-timing his girlfriend. Seems pretty obvious to me what he was getting out of it. They're all the same. All they want is to sleep with you, and if they can't, they get it somewhere else. That's you: the somewhere else."

"You're being ridiculous," Wyatt says. I'm too stunned to say anything.

"Shut up, Wyatt, this isn't about you," Rei shouts.

"Then what are we fighting about?" I scream back.

"I don't care, you know. I don't care about him. What I care about is that you would go behind my back, after everything I've done for you, and try to steal my boyfriend."

"I'm leaving," Wyatt says. He stomps off, but Rei and I are too busy screaming at each other to process it.

"I'm not stealing your boyfriend!" I say.

"I *literally* just heard you. And I see you flirting with him. You got cheated on, so you think you get a free pass?"

"No one is cheating with anyone!"

"Ladies," X breaks in.

"Stay out of this!" we shout. He retreats back into the garage with Lani and Trinity.

"I'm in love with him and he—"

"Yeah, and he's in love with you! Or he would be if you would stop acting like this."

"But he doesn't want someone like me. He wants someone who knows what food stamps look like. Someone who has parents like his. He thinks I'm a spoiled rich brat."

"Because you are, Rei! You are a stuck-up rich brat sometimes!"

"It's not my fault my parents are successful."

"No one said it's your fault! But, like, we can't all walk on eggshells about how much the rest of our lives are broke bullshit just because it makes you uncomfortable that you're rich. Suck it up!"

"You think people with money are evil and so you have the right to take anything you want from them, because you don't have anything. Well, just because life dealt you a bad hand doesn't mean you get to take things that don't belong to you."

"Wow. That may be the bitchiest thing you've ever said."

"You're a boyfriend stealer. That's what you are. You flirt and flirt and flirt, and you steal boyfriends because you think you're entitled to it because your life is shitty."

"Screw you! If you think I'm such a boyfriend-stealing slut, why don't you stop slumming it with me? Why do you even hang out with me?"

"I don't know!" Rei screams. And then she bursts into tears. She goes back into the garage, grabs her purse, and runs toward her car. She jumps in and peels off in that eerie Prius silence.

"What the hell was that?" X asks. I burst into tears.

chapter twenty-two

"The Itinerary" looks like this, as far as I can remember.

Midnight: Scumbucket climbs into Miho's window for several hours of R-rated birthday canoodling in designated traditional lingerie, plus cake. 3:00 a.m.: Scumbucket and Miho drive to airport for 3:30 a.m. arrival. Park in long-term parking, shuttle to the terminal. Check-in, security, terrible breakfast. Flight at 7:00 a.m. Scheduled viewing: Love Crazy, Manhattan Melodrama, *unless seat-back TVs have superior options. 3:30 p.m. California time, land in Los Angeles. One-and-a-half-hour layover. (No that's not enough time to leave and come back for In-N-Out Burger Miho you pleb!!!) 5:00 p.m. red-eye to Amsterdam, mandatory sleep, PG snuggling. 1:00 p.m. arrival the next day.*

I can keep going. I know the whole five days by heart.

I push it to the back of my mind, but I can still hear that alternate world ticking away.

It's 12:01 a.m. on my birthday, and even though I know better, I unlatch my window.

~

My friends and I blow off my training plan and go hiking all morning—*flight to LA, watching Bill and Myrna, I take a nap on his shoulder*—and Rei doesn't complain about the deviation, because she still doesn't respond to our texts. I don't care, though I wonder if she regrets getting me my birthday present early. I mean, if she wants to be a paranoid plastic, so be it. Wyatt comes, but he doesn't really talk to anyone. He seems sad.

After what Rei said, I don't know how to talk to him anymore either. I wonder if I *was* flirting with him. I didn't mean to. I just wanted him to feel like he belonged, because he did. He *does.* It's like there's an awkward wall between us now, and no matter what either of us meant, it all means something different now.

We go to Uncle Tua's for lunch—*layover, walking the terminal with his hand in my back pocket*—and he makes me an ice cream cake with eighteen candles in it. We come home—*finally taking off, he's so excited by the way the buildings look like a tiny train set*—and Dad cooks his famous barbecue for everyone. My neighbors went in together and got me some very, *very* nice yellow running shoes with big cushy soles, perfect for a marathon. Dad holds my present behind his back and reveals it with a flourish: *1001 Things Every College Student Needs to Know.*

Subtle. I roll my eyes, but I'm laughing. It's still got the big clearance sticker on it, and in this moment I can see that we are exactly the same kind of stubborn, exactly the same kind of funny. Maybe it's genetic.

But then, with his other hand, he pulls out something I didn't even know I wanted: swim paddles. "So I asked at the store what to buy a triathlete, and they claimed these are the best gift no one thinks of. They say they make a big difference, make you a lot stronger and faster." They're not the big flat ones with plastic ties for your fingers, but special form-correcting ones I've seen online. "If you don't like them, we can return them," he says.

"I like them," I say quickly. "I love them." I don't know if you can love swim paddles, but I love that he asked someone what to buy *a triathlete.* My own dad called me that.

I am not lying when I tell everyone that I'm tired—*we laugh about the gross airplane dinner, dream of rijsttafel*—because I couldn't fall back asleep after I woke up at midnight. Everyone heads home around eight. I thank my elders and close myself into my room. I can hear them head next door to Mr. Oshiro's house, where they crowd into his tiny living room and put on a baseball game and shout at the television. I lie down, but it's only nine and it's still light out and I can't sleep. After an hour—*we are snuggling under thin airplane blankets*—I pull out my PlayStation from behind the fortress of books and canvases I built to keep it out of sight and out of mind, and I launch *Eldritch Codex.* My fingers automatically check Scumbucket's last log-in. He still hasn't gotten online.

I know I was secretly hoping he spent all day waiting for me in *Themria.* Like he was thinking about me all day, on his "favorite holiday," and hoping I'd telepathically know he'd meet me online, even if he couldn't be with me in person.

But no.

I don't even want to talk to him. I just want to know that he remembered. That he regrets it, even if only a little.

I notice, though, that Wyatt is on.

I send him a gram. He's unmuted me a second later. We're in different parts of *Themria,* but there's this weird fuzzy animation of him that shows up in the corner. He's a Scholar, like me, with a pretty sweet wolf familiar.

"Hey," he says. "What's up?"

"Not much, couldn't sleep."

"That sucks. Did you have a good birthday? Sorry if I made things awkward."

"You didn't. I was super tired."

"Still overtraining."

"Probably," I say. I try to think of a segue, but I can't, so I just come out and say it. "Wyatt, can you do me a favor and keep it totally secret?"

"Uh, sure," he says, and I can hear him nervously laughing, even though his avatar is currently fighting off an owl.

"Can you look up and see if this player is online?"

I text him Scumbucket's username from my phone. I hear his phone ding on the line, and his avatar pauses while he looks at it. Then some cursing, and some maneuvering to get away from the owl. His avatar hides in a cave while Wyatt is searching.

Wyatt goes quiet for a minute. I already know what he sees.

"Is he?"

"No," Wyatt says. "He was playing a few hours ago, though."

I look at my screen, where his username is still grayed out. He blocked me. That's why it looks like he hasn't been on since before we broke up. Because that's when he blocked me. It was before he even told me.

"It's him, isn't it," Wyatt says.

"Yeah."

"Clearly a Hanzo main. Want to go loot his ship?" Wyatt asks.

There are tears rolling down my face. I keep my voice steady, speaking carefully.

"No, I was only curious," I say. "I'm going to bed."

But I don't get off the line. My avatar stands staring at a wall because my hands are shaking too badly to hold the controller.

I hear Wyatt clear his throat.

"Look, I barely knew him. But I do know other guys. And, like, I know this doesn't make it better, but I've wanted to tell you this for months, but I thought you might think I was hitting on you and then Rei is so . . . well, whatever. Anyway. I wanted to say, for what it's worth . . . maybe the reason he ghosted isn't because he didn't think you were special, but because he couldn't face what he'd done."

"Do you think so?"

"Yeah, I do."

"Thank you," I say, and my voice breaks, and I hate myself for it. "Sorry, I have to go."

"Good night, Miho."

"Good night. And thanks."

~

I take his cruddy old PlayStation, wrap it in his stupid pink shirt. I take it outside and put it in the trash. It's not even worth trying to sell it. It's garbage. Crashes all the time anyway.

Screw it, I always wanted a Switch anyway.

I take a bath. It feels good to be clean. I haven't been out of a sports bra in weeks. When I shower, I only have the energy to shave my legs or wash my hair, so I am always spiky or full of knots. I am missing two toenails. It doesn't hurt exactly, but it looks super weird. I put on my favorite fancy lace socks, just for fun.

When it's almost midnight—*we are over the Atlantic*—I open the top drawer of my dresser and dig to the bottom, under all the practical, period-stained-but-still-wearable panties, under my flock of sports bras, to Rei's hand-me-down lingerie.

Why am I doing this? I wonder. My hands reach into the drawer and take out both pieces, top and bottom. They are almost weightless, and it's like someone else is pulling the strings as I slip them on.

I tell myself I'll take it off in a second, that it doesn't mean anything. I know I'm lying.

The lingerie fits differently than before. Not better or worse, just different. My legs are weirdly big. My arms, though, put Michelle Obama's to shame. I flex a bicep. I raise my eyebrows at the resulting wave from under my skin. I'm a badass—look at those biceps! I've been so busy training, I haven't even had time to ponder this new eruption of abs, which are almost visible under a layer of fat. If I lean just right, I can see the muscles. When did these show up?

But then he's in my head again. *Is this what he likes?* I wonder. This tiny, tight body stripped of fat? He's the only person who could say whether my body is as nice as hers.

It shouldn't matter.

And it *doesn't.*

I force myself to look again. I shake out my 3C curls, which for whatever reason are drying perfectly tonight. They look cool and bouncy. I use my fingers to style them a little, throw in a few bobby pins and a bow.

I take a step back, strike a stupid pose, hands on hips, giant biker legs standing strong. I look so much like me. There's the bruise from this week's ill-executed bike mount. I have superbad tan lines right where my bike shorts hit, and all over my back in crisscrossing patterns from my five different swimsuits. I look at the spot I burned being a dumbass, trying to get pizza out of Uncle Tua's pizza oven without a glove for the billionth time. I never learn. I didn't become someone else. Just another me. It makes me smile.

I have the window open, and it's oddly cold for July. Hawai'i cold, at least. I should latch it. I look out that window and think about Rei, about Satan. I think about who was supposed to come through that window at 12:00 a.m. on the dot. I look at my phone. I've been checking it all day. Not a word. Not a *single word.* Not even, I don't know . . . "Sorry"?

It's 12:01.

I lie down and stare at the ceiling.

That's it. It's over.

I wonder what I'll be doing next year on my birthday. I'll know where I'm going to college. I'll have done an Ironman . . . well, a Miho-man. I mean, I sure hope so. One month to go. I hope I can pull this off. I've worked so hard. And I'm 100 percent confident I can finish. Okay, 97.6 percent. But I'm also so, so scared.

Miho, age nineteen. Hard to imagine.

Well, not that hard. It's not like I don't know what I wish for.

I sit up.

It seems so obvious at 12:01.

I reach into my desk and grab a piece of paper. Right across the top I write, "The Itinerary."

Midnight, Miho's 19th Birthday. Miho can't sleep because she's too excited. She's all packed. She watches movies until 4:00 a.m.

She gets a ride from her dad to the airport. Her dad is proud of her.

She gets on the plane.

She goes to Amsterdam.

And I will. I know it. And I'll stand there and see my crows, and I'll be the person I've been dreaming of becoming my whole life. I'll see things I never imagined for myself all by myself. I don't need him for that. And I'll do the things I want to do. And I will finish a freaking Ironman. And I will apply to art school and know all 1001 things every college student needs to know, and I will do these things because I am amazing. I *am* amazing. I *am.*

I'm going to live the itinerary I am making today.

chapter twenty-three

It was only a matter of time. My phone lights up with a message.

"Can you meet me somewhere?"

I smile, and my heart feels so full, because real love is like that: it doesn't disappear.

"When?" I text.

"Tomorrow 9 a.m."

"Where?"

"The Marriott downtown."

"The Marriott? The hotel? Upgrade to our normal trysts."

"The Marriott."

"Just making sure it's not autocorrect."

"I missed you."

I text X that I'll be missing my run tomorrow.

I can't stop smiling.

I wait in front of the Marriott because it's kind of a nice hotel, so I don't want to go in the lobby. It's hot, and I'm nervous and jittery because I skipped my run, and biking over here doesn't cut it anymore. I'll make it up later. This is more important. I feel arms wrap around me from behind. I missed this so much.

"I'm sorry."

I turn around and hug her.

"No, Mi-kins, honestly. I'm sorry," Rei says again, holding me by the shoulders. "Wyatt won't even answer my messages he's so mad."

"He has a right to be."

"I know," she says. Part of me wants him to forgive her, and part of me wonders if he should. Wyatt and I, we're not a thing, we never have been a thing, we aren't going to be a thing. But when your friends aren't right for each other, and you like them both, what do you say? Maybe you say nothing. Maybe you have to let them figure it out on their own, and try to love them both.

"You left us hanging for a month, Rei," I say, because it needs to be said.

"I don't know what I was thinking," she says. "I needed some time to get my head straight. And then after that, I was too ashamed to say anything. It never seemed like the right time. And then finally I got this sign, like your 'Anything Is Possible' banner—"

"I wanted to text you, but I wasn't sure what you wanted when you stopped answering," I say, cutting her off.

"I know you weren't sneaking around with Wyatt."

"You can still see my phone."

"No. That was ridiculous. I'm so sorry. It's just, I get jealous. I always have. Jealous of you and X, jealous of Wyatt and the imaginary person I made up for him to cheat on me with. I hate feeling like I'm the one in our set that doesn't belong because of money or whatever. I can't take what I said back, but if you can find it in your heart . . ."

But I don't have the patience to listen to her apologize all flowery like she wants to. The Rei Show has more entertaining episodes I want to see. The ones where we go to the mall and try on clothes, and go to the beach in 1920s swimsuits. The ones where we watch HBO on her parents' flat-screen, or spend hours doing each other's hair. Even though I'm still angry, I put my arms around her because she's Rei and I love her, and even if she feels like she's on the outside looking in, I know she's not.

"I've worn your underwear, Rei," I say when I finally let her go. "That's a bond that can't be broken."

~

We sit outside the Marriott for a while, catching up, waiting for something. I'm not sure what it is we're waiting for until X pulls up.

"What are you doing here?" I ask.

"Rei invited me to come consult."

"I invited you because I'm about to show off. I got Miho the greatest late birthday present of all time, and we're going to go pick it up."

"You already got me an early birthday present."

"And if you merge an early birthday present with a late birthday present, they average out to a birthday present delivered on your birthday, that I wish I hadn't missed."

"You don't have to buy me things," I say.

"Well, if we're being honest, it was a gift to myself."

I raise my eyebrow at X. He shrugs. He genuinely has no idea what's going on.

We go into the hotel, and all the signs in the lobby say MULTISPORT FITNESS EXPO. It's packed. We follow Rei, struggling to stay together in the crowd, until we reach a space bigger than my high school's gym. It's blocked off with curtains. Behind them, it sounds like a carnival. People are laughing and talking.

We line up. Everyone around us is an adult. I make myself remember that technically, I'm an adult too. Still, I huddle a little closer to X. A woman scans a QR code on Rei's phone. She hands us some lanyards, which we shove in our pockets, and we head through the curtain.

"Welcome to triathlon heaven," Rei says.

"Whoa," I say.

Inside, there's a million different booths. I see a weird little pool set up for "wet suit testing," and at another, a very underdressed lady is giving out samples of an energy drink. There are booths for every schmancy bike brand I can name. A lecture about hydration. Professional athlete signings. Bikes *everywhere.*

I see everything in here so differently than I would have at the beginning of the summer. I recognize the cone-shaped helmets as aero helmets, and those shoe covers I used to think looked like moon boots. I know what a trisuit is, chamois butter, arm warmers, why you would need special sunglasses, what all of these strange bumpy rollers are for. I have questions for that expert who's speaking about periodization, about critical swim speed. I recognize all the training toys I'd love to try out, all the bizarre metrics that Wyatt's a huge nerd for. What would we learn if we had a heart rate monitor, a power meter? How good could I be? Could I be great at this? Who knows.

I'm surprised more by what I do know than what I don't.

Who cares if we're the only kids here. These are my people. This is freaking awesome.

"I have to go on a secret mission," Rei says.

"I'm going to go find the gents," X says.

"I'm going to go spend every dollar I have," I say.

"Meet back here in fifteen?" Rei asks.

"Deal," X says.

"Deal." I practically float away from them toward the glorious tri nerd market.

My eyes scan the logos on the canopies. I notice Pipeline Tri Club's flower in a bike wheel. The charity bike they're giving away is standing on a pedestal under a spotlight. That Corneille time trial bike is a thing of beauty. I do want to at least sniff around it. Possibly lick it. Haven't decided.

I make a beeline for the booth. Maybe I should join their club. Then I would still have a club even after my friends are gone. I'm a little younger than most of them, but I looked online and you only have to be eighteen, and the dues aren't bad. I almost signed up online, but I got so shy thinking about showing up. I wondered if they'd look at me, look at my junky bike, and think, *You?*

But hey, everyone's gotta start somewhere.

As I'm walking to check it out, I spot the most bizarre bike I've ever seen. I do a double take. I look at my phone. I've got fifteen minutes.

I approach the booth like a moth to the flame. One bike is all angles. Another doesn't have a seat tube. Sharp bikes that look like one giant knife, like you're cutting into the wind.

They're called "concept bikes." I've seen them online. It makes you wonder what's possible. There are all kinds of regulations on road bikes you ride in races. But these are bikes without anyone saying "you can't." I'm fascinated.

Except.

There's a security guard looking at me.

I see him out of the corner of my eye, hovering. He's in a brown uniform. Hotel security.

No, he's not watching me. I'm being paranoid. He's doing his job. He's looking around.

I am wearing black sweatpants that I cut off at the knee and an "Uncle Tuba" T-shirt with the sleeves ripped off. My hair got sweaty under my helmet on the ride over here, and I didn't bother to fix it. I have a gym bag full of sweaty clothes from my ride over that probably makes me look a little like I might be homeless.

I smooth my hair down. It springs right back up.

I look again.

He *is* watching me.

No, no, no.

I make myself turn around and look at the bike. It's like Rei is always saying: I *feel* like I don't belong, but that's just a feeling. This is exactly like J. Crew. I get to be here, same as anyone else. I should be enjoying myself. I *am* enjoying myself.

"Miss?"

I don't turn around. There are a lot of misses here.

I feel a hand on my shoulder.

"Miss? Can I see your badge, please?" the voice asks.

I turn around. It's the guard. He doesn't look angry or cruel. He looks like they all look: suspicious. They're trained to see things that don't belong. That's their job.

But, joke's on him: I belong here. I have a ticket. I have every right to be here. So what if I'm the only teenager I see and everyone around me is a middle-aged, super-skinny white guy. Except, I'm not the *only* girl here. I'm not the *only* person who isn't white. The whole Pipeline Tri Club is right there in the corner, and they're almost all women of color. There are a few others. So why me? Why did he single me out?

Wait, badge?

"My what?"

"Your *badge.* This is a private event."

"Oh, my . . . my badge," I say. I am so freaked out that my hands are shaking. He must mean that thing on a lanyard that Rei handed me. Where did I put it? I open my bag and look desperately inside. The stench from the clothes I wore to bike over here hits us both in the face, but I dig deeper. I have so much food in here, because I'm hungry all the time, that it absolutely looks like I've been living out of this bag. I glance up. He's seeing exactly what I'm seeing, smelling exactly what I'm smelling.

"You're not allowed to be here," he says.

"What?"

"Without a badge, you're not allowed to be here."

"But I—"

I stutter out a few more things while I look for it. The guard rolls his eyes, knowing I'm looking for a badge I couldn't possibly have. I look up. I'm about to start crying.

"There's no need to make a scene. Could you please come with me?" the man asks. He puts his hand on my shoulder.

Everyone's eyes are on me.

I want to disappear.

I am sitting in the manager's office alone. The security guard deposited me here while he went to find his boss. I am crying now, dumping my entire bag on the floor. His words echo in my head. "You're not allowed to be here."

I give up on my bag and start checking my pockets. I feel it immediately. It's in my right-hand back pocket. I was too panicked to think of that when he yanked me off the floor. I give a sigh of relief as the door opens.

The man who steps in isn't wearing a uniform. He's in a normal suit. He's going bald, but he looks friendly.

"I found it," I shout. "It was in my pocket."

"Oh?" says the manager. "Can I see?"

I hand it to him. He gives my badge a cursory glance, then hands it back.

"Second door on the left down the hall, then take the elevator back down," he says, pointing to the door.

"That's . . . that's it?" I ask. He laughs, and his smile makes me smile, like a defensive reflex.

"What were you expecting?"

"I don't know," I say. "I thought it was more . . . serious, I guess."

He helps me gather my things up off the floor where I dumped them.

"No, you're not in trouble. The organizers have our staff being extra vigilant because there's a lot of expensive junk out there," he says. "You doing one of these, uh, triathlons?"

"Yes," I say quietly. Too quietly. He laughs at me again.

"I'm sorry we scared you, kiddo. Go out there and have fun. Just keep your badge visible."

"Thanks." I clutch my bag to my chest and head for the door. But something makes me turn back around. He's already settled into his desk.

"Why . . . me?" I ask.

"What?" he asks, looking up.

"Why did that guard pick me?"

"Oh, didn't they tell you at the door? Security's supposed to make sure everyone's got their badges."

"Nobody else was wearing a badge."

The manager pauses. He stands up from his desk. He comes around to the front of it, then leans back, crossing his arms. I cower a little, like somehow he's threatening me.

He gestures to me with two fingers, and it's like I can't disobey him, even though I know I don't have to do what he says. He's just some hotel manager. I could turn around and run away. But I'm too terrified to do anything but walk toward him.

I stand in front of him, like a kid about to get scolded.

"Now, look. Nobody 'picked' you. You weren't wearing a badge. Our guards have instructions to make sure only ticketed guests have access to that space. If you had found your badge and showed it to him, he would have gone on to someone else."

"But no one was wearing a badge. And I didn't see him ask anyone else."

"The fact that you didn't see it doesn't mean it didn't happen."

"But he was watching me," I say. I don't know why I'm still talking. I just want him to say it. I want him to admit to me what happened, so I can believe it myself.

I know what happened.

That guard saw someone who didn't belong here. Someone in cruddy clothes, with messy hair, who wasn't a skinny white guy. He knew I wasn't the kind of person who did triathlons. He knew I wasn't like all the other people around me.

I know it. I don't even want him to *do* anything, I just need someone to *say it.*

"Look, kid," the manager says, his voice low. "What you're saying, it's a serious accusation. Now, we had a misunderstanding. See? I'm saying we had a simple *misunderstanding.* I'm apologizing to you for the inconvenience. But my guy did nothing wrong. You were not *'profiled'* or *'singled out.'*" He makes air quotes, and you can almost hear his eyes rolling. "The rules say you have to wear your badge. You're welcome here same as everybody, but make sure your badge is visible."

"But no one else was wearing their badge! Why did he pick me—"

"Do you want to get this guy fired? Is that what you want? You want to ruin a man's life because you had to spend, what, five minutes in this office? I know where you're going with this. You want to turn this into an 'incident,' right? You want to say this was some kind of racist thing. But the truth is, my employee was trying to keep everybody *safe.* He's a normal guy, doing his job. And if you pursue this, if you make me file an incident report, he's going to be unhirable. He will be out of a job before you can blink, because this hotel does not tolerate discrimination. We are a family establishment, and we strive to provide a welcoming environment for every guest."

I can't speak. He's talking real quiet, like someone might overhear us. He leans back, and I get smaller as he looks at me.

"So what do you want to do, kid? We're all happy now, right? You go back out and enjoy yourself. No harm done."

I bite my lip. He's right. No harm done. What did I lose, sitting here in this office?

"Yeah," I say. "Yeah, cool. No harm done."

But as the manager ushers me out of his office, my face is burning, and my heart is pounding. I get off the elevator, and I know people are staring. Maybe they're not. Maybe I should have been wearing my badge. But even now, no one is wearing theirs. I pull mine out of my pocket and hang it around my neck. Rei and X are waiting, looking around for me.

"Where did you get off to?" Rei asks. She's got a box in her arms.

"I need to go," I say.

"What happened?" X asks.

"Nothing, it was . . . a *misunderstanding,*" I say.

~

We're all the way to my bike chained up outside the hotel before X and Rei manage to wrangle the story out of me.

Even as I'm telling them about that dick manager and the racist security guard, I'm defending them: "He probably didn't consciously pick me out because I look different," and "The manager was nice, but . . ."

X gives me a hug. He gets it. When Rei finally gets the gist of it, the first thing she does is pull out her phone. "What are you doing?" I ask. "Calling our lawyer," she says, and I have to beg her to let it go. I don't want that security guard to lose his job. Because it's never the manager who gets fired. It's the people who are disposable. People like my dad, like me.

I hate being the better person. And maybe I'm *not* the better person. Maybe a lot of security guards have to get fired in order for there to be real change. But that security guard is a person, like me, and that manager put his job in my hands. *He will be unhirable.* How is that my problem? And yet it is now. And that's unfair.

Right now I feel like: if I could stay in my place, everything would be fine. Why do an Ironman? Why go to college? Why stay on this constant climb when I could just . . . not?

I sigh. I don't mean that.

I need to get on my bike and go as fast as I can. I will let myself be sad and burn it all away so I can try again tomorrow. My legs are shaking, refusing to let me clip into my pedals. I finally get moving and start pedaling up the street, shouting my goodbyes.

"Miho, wait!" Rei yells. X runs after me.

"I'm sorry," I shout back, forcing myself not to cry. "It was a good surprise, but I have to go, I'm sorry."

"Miho, watch out!"

Too late, I see the eyes of the driver as he looks up from his phone.

Then I feel the bumper of the car.

chapter twenty-four

I was in the right. I lie in the grass, shaking my head to clear the ringing.

I was in the right. It was a stop sign. He ran through it.

I was in the right.

But what does it matter when my bike is a mangled heap of metal?

I lie down.

It's over.

I hear muttering all around me, that melting-pot sound spiced up with expletives in twelve languages. I'm not hurt. Got the wind knocked out of me. I can hear X asking me something as I sit up, but I'm only half listening. Rei is crying. The driver sped away on one flat tire. That's what I get from Rei. The crowd of people around us is asking if I'm okay, but I only have one thought running through my mind: *my bike.*

"Can one of you grab my bike?" I manage to get out as soon as I find my breath. No one moves.

A woman sprints over to me. I recognize her from inside. She has a shirt on with the flower in the bike wheel. The Pipeline Tri Club.

"Sit down," the woman says, and I do. "I'm a paramedic," she tells the crowd.

"Oh god, oh god," Rei is saying. I realize that my hair is wet near my ear. I touch my hair, and my hand comes away covered in blood. As soon as I see it, I'm nauseous.

"Okay, honey," the woman says. "We're calling an ambulance."

"No!" I shout. "Don't!"

"You were hit by a car," the woman says.

"Please, my friend will drive me to the hospital. I can't afford an ambulance," I say. If she calls this ambulance, I might be on the hook for thousands of dollars. That's the emergency here. I grab her arm. "I feel fine. I was wearing my helmet and everything. I think I just scraped myself and got the wind knocked out of me. I'm good."

She looks me over, hesitating with her phone.

"Are you serious? She's in shock! Call the ambulance!" Rei says.

"I'm eighteen. I'm an adult. I'm saying don't do it because I can't pay," I tell her, talking over Rei. I slide my accent. "Please, Auntie."

She looks at me, then at Rei. She shakes her head, clucking her tongue, sliding her phone away.

"Screwed-up country, kids afraid to call 911 because of medical bills. Okay, as long as it's not serious, your friend can drive you. Take off your helmet."

I do as she says. She turns my head to the side, looking at the spot I think I'm bleeding from. It's along my chin. I must have bumped it. She grabs a bandanna from her pocket and puts it over the spot. "Hold it there. Press hard. Can you keep your head still and follow my finger with your eyes?" she asks. She makes me shrug my shoulders, touch my nose. She asks about tingling in my hands, whether I feel nauseous, and a hundred other tasks I perform like my life depends on it.

"What's your name?" she asks at last.

"Miho," I say.

"Miho what?"

"Miho Embarrassed-As-Hell."

"That's good. If your pride's broken, you probably didn't break much else. What were you doing before you got hit by the car?" she asks.

"What?" I ask. Am I in trouble for even being here?

"Concussions cause memory loss," X explains. "Tell her about the expo."

"You were here for the convention?" she asks. "You the triathlete, or a friend?"

"It's me, yes," I say with as much confidence as I have ever mustered. A very expensive ambulance is riding on this. "I've been training for my first Ironman. Well, sort of an Ironman."

She looks at me like she thinks I might have hit my head pretty hard after all, despite my excellent finger-following skills. "Well, see, my friends and I are putting on our own Ironman because the race is so expensive. So technically, it's an Iron-length race. Except I think my bike . . ." I look at X. He looks over his shoulder, then shakes his head. "I might be screwed. I think my bike is trashed."

"What kind of bike do you have?"

"I don't even know," I say. Then I realize my mistake. "Not, like, I don't know because I have a concussion. I don't know because it was painted so many times. It was secondhand." What could I say that would convince her I'm thinking clearly? My whole brain sparks to life. "My dream bike, though, is a Corneille road bike. I like the R-450 pro, particularly. I know I'd be more aerodynamic on a time trial bike, but a road bike is more versatile. Based on what I've read, clip-on aero bars are nearly as good, and then I can ride it out with my friends for fun, instead of only for triathlon. If I could only have one bike, that would be it."

"Smart thinking, for a first-timer," she says. "People spend so much money on a tri bike, it's perverse."

"I know. How can a Cervélo P5X cost more than a car?"

"Eh. Luxury sports. It's a love/hate relationship," she says. "Tell me you wouldn't ride the hell out of it if you had the chance, though, right?"

"True."

"I'd prefer a deluxe Ventum. Custom paint, integrated storage, featherlight." She sighs. "Truth is, you can only buy so much speed. When you get right down to it, it's all about putting in the time. I'd buy myself more training time over a fancy bike any day. First time I placed in my age group, I was riding an old lugged steel frame from the seventies."

"For the full?"

"Half."

"So concussion?" Rei asks impatiently. It makes me weirdly happy that she has no idea what we're talking about.

"You're okay," the woman says. "Now, you're going straight to a doctor, yes?"

"Yes," Rei and I say.

"You might need stitches," she says. "But you'll live to bike another day."

chapter twenty-five

Dad meets us at the clinic. I make him wait with Rei and X. He barely says anything, not there, not on the way home.

I don't need stitches. I get some weird glue put on the cut to close it up. It wasn't half as bad as it looked; mostly grass stains. My helmet took most of it. My bike did not fare so well. The front fork is destroyed. One of the wheels is missing and the other is bent. The top tube is clearly cracked in half. I think if I'd been on a carbon frame, it might have shattered. It's a miracle I landed in the grass and rolled. I shiver thinking about what would have happened if I'd hit the pavement.

Dad puts the bike in the back of the pickup. Even I have to admit it's not worth fixing.

At home, I take my bloody bandanna and set it on my desk. It's printed with flowers and bike wheels. Even though I'm not concussed, I'm not feeling awesome. No tri club for me. Not without a bike. No pizza deliveries. No race.

The whole house creaks, and I know from the groaning floor that all my uncles are right outside my door.

"Miho?" Mr. Bu asks from outside. I steel myself and open the door. My room is too small to invite them in. We stand awkwardly.

"We're sorry about your accident," Mr. Oshiro says.

"But don't you worry. We are going to go right out and get you a new bike. A better one than before," Mr. Kalani says.

"You don't have to do that," I say. And then, because I can't help myself, I ask: "How?"

"Well . . . we haven't figured that out yet," Mr. Oshiro says. "But we will. A *really* nice one. We promise."

"Thank you," I say. They have no idea what a nice bike is, because if they knew, they wouldn't make a promise I know they can't keep. But it's my best shot, and I'm grateful.

"We'll let you rest," Mr. Bu says. They shuffle away toward the door, whispering. Once the screen door closes, I hear Dad approaching.

"Dad, I'm going to bed. My brain hurts."

"Did your uncles tell you?"

"About what?"

"The bike," he says. "And anything else you need. New helmet. Whatever got broken."

I smile despite myself.

"So all it takes to wring money out of you is a hit-and-run?"

"Miho—"

"No, it's fine. I know we can't afford it."

Dad's jaw drops, but he closes it. He crosses his arms.

"You listen to me, my flower. If your uncles say that there will be a bike at this race, there will be a bike at this race. You keep training. Don't worry about the bike," he says. "And don't you ever, *ever* let me hear that you didn't call an ambulance when you were hurt. Ever. If it's an emergency, you call a goddamn ambulance. You go straight to the hospital. Do you hear me?"

"But it would have cost a thousand dollars!"

"Then I would have paid a thousand dollars."

"You don't have a thousand dollars!"

"I don't care about the money, Miho! Do you know how much it scares me that you hesitated?"

"I'm sorry!"

"No. I'm sorry. Because I thought I was clear. Your life matters so much more to me than debt. Don't you ever do that again. I'm sorry I made you feel like we don't have enough money for the things that matter. So if I have to buy you a helmet, and a triathlon bike, and whatever else you need to do this thing in order to prove that to you, I will find a way to buy those things. Because I cannot believe that you would worry about the cost of an ambulance when it's a question of your life. That *terrifies* me."

We sit in silence for what feels like hours. Except Achilles. He's totally spoiling the atmosphere of serious family interaction by trying to get Dad to throw something for him, yipping with increasing desperation.

"You don't have to buy those things," I say at last. "I'm sorry. But I didn't need an ambulance. It was a tiny cut."

"I know. But next time."

"I promise," I say.

"Good."

"I'm going to bed," I say. Dad turns to go. But when he is halfway down the hall, he shouts after me.

"I'm serious. Don't you worry about the bike."

"Good night, Dad," I say.

"Good night, my flower."

I close the door.

I slide into bed.

Maybe I should quit.

For a split second it feels so good to give up. My muscles relax as I imagine no more VO2 max sessions, no more hill sprints, no more descending 100s. Everything is one foot in front of another, but eventually, that's a lot of steps. You get tired.

My phone lights up: X.

"No run tomorrow. 2 days required break for glue according to the internet. No swim until it's legit healed, but Wyatt is bringing over his swim cord things for dryland swim."

My legs twitch. I already want it.

"My uncles are trying to find me a bike," I text back. "But if they can't . . . dunno."

"Trin thinks you can use my brother's bike. She is working on it. Three other options lined up."

"Roger that." In my crew, there are enough sisters and

brothers and cousins that there's got to be something with two wheels. It's just a bike, after all. All it really has to do is roll.

I take a breath. An unplanned recovery day. Then it's time for the next step. For now, bed.

The three dots appear.

"Avengers marathon instead?"

"Thin Man," I insist. "Haven't done that since we were in middle school."

"It's a date."

chapter twenty-six

Two weeks since the accident. Two weeks before my race. I'm stuck waiting tables every shift because of this idiotic "tapering" thing where you rest before a big race. You're not supposed to ride so much. I still don't have a bike, so that's no problem. I can't believe I'm going to say this, but I am aching for a twenty-mile run. Now that I have a fueling strategy and Lani's candy, running that far makes me feel invincible. I know I shouldn't, but I sprint hard on my easy runs to burn off some panic. *Save it,* I tell myself. *Save it for the race.* But I look at the numbers and my heart flutters in disbelief.

I slide through my easy swims. I do a few loops on X's brother's little mountain bike, which is almost my size and the best option we found. I can make this work, I think. It'll hurt, but I can make it work, if it comes to that.

I'm losing my mind. It's called "taper madness" because I'm addicted to all those miles. My mind wonders things I know my best self doesn't care about. I compulsively check the weather. I google so many weather what-ifs that the ads on my phone change to specialized emergency preparedness kits, like the one Mr. Oshiro has hidden away for the apocalypse, full of nutritional paste and canned food. I started making packing lists for my special needs bags a week ago.

But no matter how much I want to, I don't fall down that black hole back into sadness.

I know this is the taper talking.

Still. There is one *real* problem. 112 miles on a souped-up kiddie bike? That's not bricolage, that's batshit.

I trust my uncles. They say there will be a bike, there will be a bike. It can't be worse than my old one.

But I worry.

~

One week to go. I sit outside Tua's, waiting for Dad to pick me up. When he arrives, my uncles are in the car with him, packed in tight.

"Why?" I ask.

"You'll see," he says, and my heart jumps.

"But there's no room," I say.

"There's room," he says, and I roll my eyes and climb into the back, where I'm squashed between Mr. Bu and Mr. Kalani. "Worked better when you were littler."

Squished between them and tired from my shift, I don't notice where we're headed until we pull up outside Kyle's bike shop. As I'm getting out of the car, I see Rei's Prius, X's car, and Lani's scooter. And the lights are on, even though it's definitely after closing.

"Oh my god. Uncles," I say.

"We told you there would be a bike," Mr. Oshiro says. "A *nice* bike."

I won't get my hopes up. But Kyle said there might be a used bike.

Keep your hopes low, I command myself.

There's a small army of bikes hanging out on the porch, and one woman sitting on the steps watching them. I recognize her.

"Miho?" she asks. "How's the head?"

"It's you!" I say. The paramedic, I realize.

"Anita," she says. "Glad you're okay. Go on in, you're late."

"For what?"

"You'll see."

When I get inside, the bike store is packed with my friends, uncles, and women from the tri club. And in the middle of it all is a Corneille R-450 Pro in sky blue.

"We entered on your behalf," Mr. Bu says. "Got it right under the deadline. And you won!"

"No way," I say.

"Yes way," says a woman who is walking around in her bike kit and bike shoes, waddling with her toes out so she doesn't slip. "Hi. I'm Aaliyah. I'm the president of the Pipeline Tri Club."

"I'm Miho. I'm . . ."

I'm completely tongue-tied.

"We heard you need it for a special race, and we managed to get the company to send the bike early."

"But it was a tri bike. In the posters."

"Seems like you met one of our members already," Aaliyah says. "She made a good case for the road bike, and the company agreed."

"Oh my god. Oh my *god,*" I say, and it's all I can do to keep myself from clapping like a seal.

"One thing," Aaliyah says. "Corneille wants to do a promotion on social media about the recipient of their charity bike. So, we'll do a few pictures now, and their photographer will catch up with you and do a fun promotional shoot sometime in the next few weeks. And we need a few pictures from your race day."

"And that's it?"

"That's it. The bike is yours."

"Oh my god," I say again, my hands over my mouth so I stop sounding so stupid. I lift them to let out a "thank you."

"Here, let's do the picture before she drools on it," Kyle says. "Everyone over there around the bike. Here's your sign, Miho."

"Sign?"

"Yeah, here. Just hold it and—Trinity, you stop making that face."

"Sorry," Trin says. As Kyle is wrangling the others into the frame, I look at the sign I'm holding. It reads THIRD ANNUAL RECIPIENT OF THE CORNEILLE CHARITY TRIATHLON BIKE. It's huge. That's me, I think. *Recipient. Charity.* When I'm holding it, it'll be like a label right over me.

And I just. I just.

"Wait," I say. Everyone turns to look at me, and I feel very small. "Thank you so much for everything. But I can't take charity."

I hand the sign back.

"What?" Kyle asks.

"I'll buy a bike," I say. "The best bike I can afford. I'd rather pay my own way."

"Miho, you apologize right now," Dad says. "You are being ungrateful."

"No, I am grateful," I say. I turn to Aaliyah. "I am. I truly am. And when I have a bike that I've *earned,* I want to join your club. But I can't do this as charity. I want to deserve the things I have."

"Miho!" Dad says. He turns to Aaliyah. "I am *so* sorry. She doesn't mean it."

"Don't apologize for her," she says. "She's a full-grown woman."

"It's a beautiful, beautiful bike," I say, touching it longingly. "But people are going to think I got so many things I didn't deserve. They'll say, oh, she never would have gotten into that school if she had been a white kid. Or, she never would have gotten that job on her own—it was a diversity hire! No matter how great I am, I'm going to hear that for the rest of my life. I need my finish line to be something I earned, like anyone else. And for me, that includes the bike."

Aaliyah smiles.

"You know, Miho, I just met you, but I get it. I do. I've been there. It's important to be proud of yourself, to feel like you've got dignity. And if taking charity makes you feel not proud, then you don't have to take it. But let me tell you something. A rich girl? She *wins* a bike like this? She doesn't worry about it being charity. She feels *lucky.* She feels like, hey, I won! Guilt is a poor girl's game."

"I'll be a charity case," shouts one of the women.

"Me too," another says. "This bike is way nicer than mine."

"Hell, I'd take this charity bike," Aaliyah says. "Charity, it isn't always a bad thing. When you get 'charity' to go to school, like I did, like most people here did, that's the school paying for what they want. They want *you.*" She points at me. "Same with this bike. We are so committed to getting girls like you into this sport, we are willing to pay you a *ten grand* bike to make it happen, Miho. We want girls with your grit, and your experience, and your ability to do the work. Think about it this way: pro athletes, they get free stuff all the time. We're *sponsoring* you."

"But you wouldn't be sponsoring me if I wasn't poor," I say. "That's what makes it charity."

X groans. "Miho, don't you get it? They are sponsoring *you.* You wouldn't be *you* if you weren't poor, or mixed, or someone who got a perfect SAT score, or an artist, or Californian, or Hawaiian, or my best friend, or a girl who spent six months having the weirdest post-breakup temper tantrum of all time."

"Not a temper tantrum, you rotten louse!"

"What I mean is, you wouldn't be you if you weren't any part of you," X says, putting a hand on the bike. "Just like any of us. Like I wouldn't be me if I wasn't poor and gay."

"And a genius," I add.

Lani puts her hand on the bike. "And I wouldn't be me if I wasn't fat."

"And the best chef in all Hawai'i," Trin says. "And I wouldn't be me if I wasn't—"

"Part feral wolf?" Lani asks.

"Scared to leave my home," she says as she puts her hand on a tire. "And Wyatt wouldn't be Wyatt if he wasn't an Eagle Scout."

"And a big loser nerd who didn't have any friends until this year," he says as he grabs the seat. "And Rei wouldn't be Rei if she wasn't—"

"Jealous and insecure," she says.

"And truly amazing," Wyatt adds quietly. She puts her hand next to his. And I see, in all these hands: I did not do this myself at all, and it's wonderful.

Aaliyah grins. "See? But as I said. I get it. So, it's up to you. You can have your pride, or you can have this race on this sweet bike. Which do you choose?"

I look at the bike. The Corneille R-450 Pro, right there, with my freaking name on it and a giant pink bow.

"Well, the bike." I grab it. "Obviously."

The whole room cheers.

~

After an eternity of adjustments, fittings, and refittings for me, and many rounds of sparkling apple cider for my friends,

Rei gives me a lift home with the bike. I keep turning around and looking at it, like it's not real, like it's not there.

When we pull up, Dad and the neighbors pile out of the truck and carry it to my porch like it'll be hurt if it touches the ground. I'm not sure why all four of them are required for this task, because it's so light I can probably lift it over my head with one arm. Before I can get out, Rei puts a hand on my arm. She leans into the back seat and pulls out a box. It's the one she picked up at the expo.

"I'm sure you know what this is," she says.

"A new power costume?"

"I went with the onesie. You should practice in it to make sure it doesn't rub anything weird."

"Just like the real athletes," I say.

"Exactly. Open it," she says. But I don't.

"Thanks, Rei. For everything. But I can't wear a costume. I can't do this as someone else. When I'm out there, I want to be me," I say.

Rei laughs.

"Mi-kins, you think I'd let you go out there as anyone but yourself? Open it."

I raise an eyebrow at her. I take the box and pull the ribbon, and the lid falls off. I look at Rei.

"Jesus, Rei."

"You're welcome," she says. She wraps her arms around me. I let the box fall to the floor of the car. There's no room for anything in this hug but us.

RACE DAY

The Starting Line

The sun is still down. I can't sleep any longer. I'm not tired. I woke up like clockwork a split second before my alarm. I'm not even sure I slept.

I have run through this routine hundreds of times. Kyle's advice was to practice not just the race but everything: going to bed, getting dressed, what I'll eat, how I'll pack my bag. It should feel like it's happened a million times before, so you can have your head in the game.

I shower and dress. "Heading out in fifteen," Dad calls. I can hear him and the neighbors loading up the truck. Mr. Bu and Mr. Oshiro are arguing about how to fit in the grill and the entire dead pig that they have disgustingly purchased.

Like a nervous tic, I grab a few extra hair ties and shove them into one of the plastic grocery bags I'm bringing. I have my swim bag, my first transition bag, my second transition bag, and my two "special needs" bags to perk me up halfway through the bike leg and halfway through the run. I put all of it into a duffel bag that cuts painfully into my shoulder and look at myself in the mirror.

Mr. Kalani cut my hair special last night. It is shorter than ever and looks amazing. *Of course* this is the day I have a good curl day, right before I shove it all up under a swim cap. I shake them out and smile. *Don't forget to smile,* X's voice in my head reminds me. I won't. I promise.

I am wearing X's hoodie and a pair of ratty sweatpants over my trisuit, bundled up against the morning. I am so zipped in that I worry I'll need to pee, and worrying makes me need to pee. But if I have to pee, then I have to pee, and I'll deal with that later. Nervous pees happen to everyone.

I have done this leaving routine hundreds of times in my head. I am zen calm under all these nerves as I walk down the hall, Achilles at my heels. I grab my breakfast bento from the fridge. I step out onto the porch. And there are the headlights, right on schedule.

"Get in!" X shouts. Lani and Wyatt are leaning out of the back seat. Rei has my bike in the Prius with Trinity. I pile in and wave to my dad.

"We'll see you down there," he says. "Just as soon as these lolos figure out this puzzle. Been playing Go for months, and can't come up with a strategy to fit two damn things in a truck."

"Will you be late?" I ask.

"We'll be there. I promise."

When we get to the beach, Rei and Trinity have already set up my transition area. It's on a tiny stretch of cement that was once meant for boats. No one but us will be out here today. Wyatt got a real permit and everything.

"We couldn't sleep," Trinity explains as she sweeps the area around the bike. I look at her quizzically, pointing to the broom. "Broken beer bottles," she explains. "People suck." Then she rolls a big sheet of something that looks like Astro-Turf out toward the water. Rei is somewhere near. I hear her singing: *". . . the world is full of zanies and fools."*

My beautiful, shiny, new, foreign, perfect bike is on a stand we borrowed from Kyle. Kyle sent his regrets. He has to work. I go over to my bike, run my hand over it. I barely got to ride it, barely had time to get used to using road bike shifters. But now that we know each other a little better, I couldn't be more in love.

Under the tiny canopy we've set up, I put out everything where I need it. I lay my towel down, just like I've practiced. I lay out my bags, shift things into order inside. I put rocks on them to keep them from blowing away. My friends will be making water and snack runs to me all day on Lani's scooter. It's sitting next to the canopy, loaded up in both panniers with water bottles, Gatorade, bananas, and Lani's homemade power chews. I open both sides, checking everything.

6 a.m. One hour to go.

I do my "activation" exercises. I jog a bit, stretch. Uncle Tua pulls up at 6:30 a.m., Dad and the neighbors in the wake of dust behind him. The boys are running the pizza shop today. They said they'd be "tracking me." I'm not sure how.

"Nervous?" X asks. I nod.

"This is the good part," Rei says, coming to join us. "All the hard stuff is over."

"It's like painting," I say. "You have to hold it all inside yourself and let it out all at once."

"Like a fart," Trinity says from behind us. Lani smacks her on the shoulder, and Trinity kisses her cheek.

"Do you feel ready?" Wyatt asks.

"I feel like standing here with you guys, I've already won." I throw my arms around X and Rei.

"That's sweet, but we've all got bets on this," Rei says. "And some of us were maybe a little specific."

"Scientific," Wyatt replies.

They keep bickering, but my head is already in the game. This stillness inside me is part of what I worked so hard for. I'm so calm. I'm so happy. I'm so ready.

~

At 6:45 a.m., I stand barefoot on the sand. It's cold without my pullover and my sweatpants. I can see the buoys Wyatt put out to keep me on course. I wish I'd gotten to swim this course beforehand, but we couldn't work it. I'm not worried. I know where I'm going. X is in the kayak, just in case. He's sitting there, sipping a thermos full of coffee. We don't talk. We don't need to.

6:50 feels a year away from 6:45. When is it going to be 7:00? I know behind me, people are getting breakfast, setting up more canopies, hooking up one of Mr. Oshiro's TVs to a generator, texting, starting the all-day process of making kalua pig. But I can't let myself listen to any of that.

Do I have to pee?

Whatever. I can pee in the water.

Stupid nervous pees.

Did I eat enough?

6:55.

What if I can't do this?

What if I screw this up?

Don't think any of that. Where's all my calm and stillness now?

6:57.

"Guys, we're going to count down," Wyatt calls back. "Come on."

I put my bare foot on the starting line. I look down. My power costume. It's a sleeveless one-piece trisuit. Rei somehow had it custom-made for me. The front panel, over my chest and up my shoulders, is yellow rising into blue. There are crows across my heart, and that dead-end road leads up into my chest. The shorts part is deep blue, with gold racing stripes up the sides. She couldn't help herself. I don't mind. On my back, between my shoulder blades, there's a silhouette of a Hawaiian crow, and all my friends' signatures around my name.

6:59.

Absolute silence. None of this feels real. They are counting down from ten. X is pulling out in the kayak. Is this really happening? My heart is pounding.

"Three . . ."

I breathe. *I am here.*

"Two . . ."

In this body. In this mind.

"One . . ."

And nothing else matters.

"GO!"

Swim

The water is cold, but I can't even feel it. I'm running, and then I'm knee-deep in the ocean and I can't run any farther, but I also can't swim yet. I crawl and scramble.

Keep it together, I tell myself. *Seconds don't matter. Your mindset does.*

I keep my eye on the buoys and let myself glide over the shallow parts, where I can touch the bottom with my hand.

And then I'm out in the open water, and everything feels right.

I can see X farther off than usual, making sure I don't get hit by a boat or drown. I have to follow the path they set out for me. It's four loops, to keep it safe, to keep it close. One *breathe,* two. One *breathe,* two. I say it in my head until I find my rhythm.

My arms burn and my back burns, but I don't think. Even in this primordial soup brain, X is there. Images pass through me without being called. Images of X, who is always in the corner of my eye. I look ahead, but he's on the horizon.

This leg's for him.

Can I pull harder? Can I go faster? Can I get under an hour?

I don't wonder. I know.

T1

My feet slip in the sand as I run out of the ocean. I fall and bang my knee on a rock. I don't even feel it. I'm up in a second, heavy with water. My legs feel like jelly. I'm panting so hard it feels like I'm breathing in burning salt. I am sprinting up the AstroTurf to my transition area.

Everyone is cheering, but I barely hear them. I'm doing exactly what I know needs to be done, exactly the way I've practiced. I throw my swim cap and goggles to one side.

"One hour and seven!" Trinity shouts at me. That's disappointing, I think. No, I'm not letting it get to me. But god I felt so fast, how did that happen? The current?

Just keep going.

I'm breathless from the swim, but I don't let myself think about it. My shoes, water, and snack are on the bike. My tiny emergency kit is in a pouch strapped to the seat post. My phone is in there in a ziplock bag. I pull on my helmet, snap it on without tying my hair. I run my bike to the start of the bike course, and for a moment I let myself look.

Everyone is cheering. X is jogging up from the kayak, shouting something.

I finally hear him.

"Go!"

Bike

This is me, in my element.

I am riding away, drinking water as I go. One foot in. Other foot in. Helmet on tight? Everything in its place? I'm good. Over my shoulder, I see Rei and Wyatt chasing me on foot and cheering. I wave over my shoulder. I have my snack. I smile.

Whatever speed I lost on the swim, I can get back on the bike. I'm not worried about it. The road is open in front of me. This is what I love. Now it's time to work. I shift myself into my comfiest gear, one that would break so many people but not me. I love that low cadence speed, that feeling of grinding, of pushing hard and smooth. I tuck in tight like a diving bird of prey, streamlined on my aero bars. I settle in. I fly.

Wyatt put markers out on the road so I'll know where I am on the bike route. 112 miles, marked every ten and at the turns. I memorized the path, but just in case. I never trained with a watch, so I didn't want one for the race. I don't want to know how I'm doing; I want to do my best in every moment. I know how this should feel at every mile, and that's what I should listen to.

I'm at Mile 20. Someone drives past me and cheers. I look up. One of the pizza boys out on a delivery, taking a picture. I wave. I chase the car.

Mile 40. Lani comes by on her scooter.

"Water call."

"Gatorade," I slobber out. I'm breathing heavy. My mouth is slimy, like my saliva is glue. I force myself to eat some energy chews and hand her the wrappers, then drink so much Gatorade.

She rides next to me as I down an entire bottle. We have to do it this way because we can't leave litter. I take two more bottles of Gatorade for the bottleholders on my bike, and I can tell that she wants to say something but won't. Only I know my body and what it needs, and even if I'm thinking with thirst, I'm the only one who can make that call now.

Then I'm alone again. I feel better. I speed up.

~

I slow down.

Mile 56. Turn and head back in.

I look down both sides of the highway. No one. I take a deep breath.

For one second, I let myself feel the solitude of an empty highway on a bike. I listen to the wind. Then I turn around.

Rei appears on the scooter to bring me my special needs bag, but I don't need anything. She knows I've got my mind on the road, and she zooms off without a word. A few miles down, I see her pulled over on the side of the road, taking pictures of me. I grin and wave, and she cheers.

I'm smiling. But my legs are killing me.

~

Mile 60. Why did I drink all that Gatorade? I need to pee.

Mile 60.5. I can't. I won't.

Mile 61. I can almost hear Trinity laughing. But good lord what a relief.

~

Mile 80. I feel it happen.

I've got a flat.

No! Front tire.

I slow to a stop and twist out of my pedals, keeping my shoes on my feet.

No. No. No. Not now!

I take a deep breath. I unzip the emergency kit. I know what to do.

My hands are shaking because I'm losing time. I pop off the wheel, squeeze all the air out, get the old tube out from under the tire. Now I'm mad. Of course this would happen. Now I'll be so slow. This bike leg is ruined.

Knock it off. Keep going.

I kneel in the grass with the wheel. My legs are jelly, and I can't stand and do this. I try to stretch the new tube onto the wheel. It won't fit.

"COME ON," I shout. It's so hard to get it on. I'm starting to cry, I'm so frustrated.

"Pull it together," I say out loud. "This is not over. You can cry or you can focus."

I take another deep breath, close my eyes, open them, and start again. Trinity made me practice this over and over. I can do this.

The tube goes on the wheel. The tire goes over. Now the CO2 cartridge. The tire inflates in an instant, exactly like it should. I feel it with my hand. Even after just one week, I know this bike by touch and feel. This is good enough to get me home.

I get the wheel back on as Trinity is riding up on the scooter. For an instant she looks concerned, and then she's all business.

"You good?"

"Good."

"Need anything?"

"No."

"I'll get the trash. Go. You got this."

As I'm riding away, I hear her howling: "We choose to go to the freaking moon!"

Mile 90. Furious about the lost time. I bike harder than I should. I bike angry.

I push against the wind, crunching myself up into a flat little glider, cutting through the universe.

Anger echoes anger. I think about everything I'm angry about, every frustration. I feel my legs getting heavier and heavier.

And then I can't help it.

He's there. His hair. His eyes. His hands. I'll never race far enough to get away from him.

All my fury becomes one question: Why? Stroke after stroke of why, burning up my legs as I battle the wind.

Why did you do it?

Why did you lead me on for so long?

Why wasn't I good enough for you to love me?

"Why" keeps my legs spinning, takes back the minutes I lost changing that tire. I have never been this fast, or this hurt, because even on *my day* he's snuck back in. I take him everywhere, like a chain that slips, throwing me off. Will he always be there waiting to jump out? Was all of this for nothing?

I fly back into camp to a cheer, but not an answer.

T2

I am shaking when I get off my bike. X is there to take it from me, and I try to run back to my transition area, but I can't. I have to walk.

Everyone crowds around me. They're all eating barbecue, and the smell makes me sick.

"You're at 5:53," Rei tells me. "You're doing great."

5:53. That means my bike time was, what, 4:40 or something?

I'm doing freaking amazing.

But things are going south.

I am walking, still walking, back to transition. I finally make it.

"Give her some room," X says, shooing everyone away. My neighbors ignore him as I'm putting on my socks and shoes.

"You can do it!"

"You are so fast!"

"Do you want a beer?"

"No!" X shouts. "Uncles!"

"Get out of the way," Dad scolds them.

X sits down next to me, and I consider asking him to help me with my shoes. But I can do it. I have to do it myself. I take a sip of water, then dump the rest of the bottle over my head.

My hands are shaking.

Tie these shoes. I'm losing time.

One foot. Just do one foot.

One foot done.

Now the other.

Done.

Now stand.

I get to my knees, and my legs will not get up. I biked too hard. I'm screwed.

X stands up as my dad comes over, and then it's just me and Dad. It's eerily quiet over by the barbecue, and I know everyone is watching. I put my face in my hands, but I'm too dehydrated to even cry.

I try to pull myself up on the pole of the tent.

It's not happening.

"Dad, I can't. I can't do it," I say. I'm frozen.

"Drink some water," he says. "Take a minute. I'm watching the time. I'll tell you when a minute is up."

I sit there for a full minute, but it feels like an hour.

"Now try," he says. I get to my knees. I wobble. I stand.

"You're wearing your nice leg," I say.

"I don't usually wear this one because it's for running. Let's go," he says. "We can start with walking."

"You can't run a marathon," I say.

"No," he says. "But I think you can."

Run

We walk for a mile, and then the walking becomes a jog.

"When did you start running?" I ask.

"You said I should try. And I thought maybe you were right."

"How often?"

"Only a few times a week," he says. "Just a few miles. I'm old. Start slow."

"Why didn't you say anything?"

"Because sometimes when you're old, you're embarrassed to try. I say to you, 'Just try college.' How can you listen to that when I won't try either? And you were right: I can do it."

"I don't know if I can do this," I say.

"Well. All you can do is try."

We run quietly for two more miles, counted out on the pavement in spray paint. At first I was dragging behind him. Now he's lagging behind me.

"You good?" he asks.

"I'm good," I say. I am. I'm running smoothly, if not fast. "Thank you. For everything. I know you don't get it, but I need this race."

"Do you remember? You said that when you started," he says, and we slow to a walk. "You said you needed this race like the wind needs the trees. And it took me all these months you've been doing this to figure out what I want to say to you."

He stops completely, panting and out of breath. I'm okay. But I stop. I need to hear this.

"I thought I'd tell you after. But I will tell you now," he says. "You are wrong about the wind."

"What do you mean?"

"You think the wind needs the trees to show people it exists? The trees are how *we* see the wind. The wind doesn't need them at all. The wind is free."

"You're right."

"You are so like the wind. Wind is created by change. Hot to cold. Wind is affected by everything on this planet. And you . . . you feel *so much.* You love *so much.* I don't understand why, but it's true. You don't need to see it in the trees to know that. You don't need to see it in this race to know that. You know it because that's who you are.

"But you *do* see it in the trees. And you *do* see it in this race. And I'm glad, because now I can see it too."

"Dad," I say. X pulls up on Lani's scooter and stops a respectful distance back. I wave at him and he rides up.

"My dad needs a lift."

"You okay?" X asks. I look at the ground. I'm standing on the marker for Mile 3. I remember when I couldn't even run this far, that day on the track.

"See you at the finish line," I say.

~

Mile 5. I'm fine. Mile 6. I'm okay. Mile 7. I'm dying. It's Lani's turn again on the bike, and she peps me up with water and energy chews, but I can barely swallow, and the idea of eating or drinking makes me nauseous. I know I have to. I take a water bottle. I'll carry it. I put snacks in my zipper pouch. Butt snacks. *Technically lower back snacks,* I hear Rei say in my head. Mile 8. I'm fine. Mile 9. I'm okay. Mile 10. I'm going down again. I have no idea how long it has been, but I'm basically walking with a half-hearted bounce. I hear my shoes scraping the pavement with every step. I can't get enough air.

My friends buzz by more often on the bike, but I wave them off every time. I don't need anything but a new pair of legs. I screwed myself by getting mad on the bike. My time is going to be terrible.

I refuse to get upset. I keep going.

~

I reach 13.1, which Wyatt has painted in pink on the sidewalk. I stop completely and look at it as I catch my breath, hands on my knees, which feel like they are full of water. There's a smudged-up drawing all around the number. My friends must have come out here with chalk last night. It's a little messed up, but I can read it. It says "You can do it." There are a few messages in languages I can't read. Uncles? I'm guessing they all say something encouraging. Mr. Kalani drew a beautiful sunflower. I hope they took a picture.

Someone, probably Trinity, drew a bunch of stick figures who appear to be running, and one lagging way behind. There's an arrow pointing to it that says "you." I laugh.

Rei drew a trophy and wrote "Cutest kit on the course award." Lani drew a cat saying "I can haz snickers?" X wrote "World's Best Talented Amateur."

I look back toward camp. I can do this.

Mile 15. Trinity delivers my special needs bag. I take everything out of it. Food, Band-Aids, everything. Then I look at it, because I don't know what I actually need. It just seems like something in there must be able to help me.

"Okay?" asks Trinity.

"I'll take this," I say, grabbing a hair tie. I have five more around my wrist. I hand everything back. At this point, my brain isn't functioning well enough to get my shoes off and on again. If my feet are bleeding, I'll have to let them bleed.

Trinity speeds off.

I hope that wasn't a mistake.

Mile 21. I have no idea where the miles in between went. My knee is bleeding. I must have tripped. Did I get more water? I don't remember. Did I eat? So much for a fueling strategy. Someone must have come by. My legs are on fire and yet feel heavier than lead. My mouth is full of scum, thick mucus I can't spit out.

But I've been here before, and pushed through it before. I know there's a place past this, and I'm strong enough to get there. I don't *think* I can. I *know* I can.

I can be here and miserable and in pain as long as I need to be.

It's okay. I am okay.

For the first time, I realize I'm alone.

There's no one here with me, in my head. There's nothing I'm keeping out, because there's nothing there. Some miles back, everything fell away. I didn't even notice. The thing I thought I was racing toward is gone. It isn't him.

And it isn't college, it isn't being a painter, it isn't traveling.

What I'm looking for isn't at the finish line. It's here. I'm looking for here, *right now,* feeling this strong. Feeling complete. I'm not racing toward *anything.* I'm just racing. And it's perfect.

I can do this. I will.

The hills around me are painted in brushstrokes that are mine. The road I see is not a dead end but a beginning. My wheat fields are around me. My crows are flying. And I'm the wind, making it all come alive.

~

My legs are heavy. I can't hear anything but my own breathing, nearly gasping.

I see X and Rei holding either side of the yellow finish-line tape. Wyatt is looking at his watch, swinging his arm wildly. Lani and Trinity are jumping up and down. My neighbors and Tua are applauding and shouting. Dad is standing with his arms crossed, watching me, back in his duct-taped plastic leg. *Stubborn,* I think.

It is a quarter mile. My legs are quaking. It is yards. My heart hurts. It is feet.

It is mine.

Recovery

I thought I'd pass out two feet past the finish line, but I need to move. My adrenaline is so high I know I'll never sleep again.

11 hours. 14 minutes. That's me. I am 11 hours and 14 minutes and all the work it took to get there and so much more.

I'm wearing the yellow finish-line tape around my neck. I am soaked. Trinity needed to dump an entire container of Gatorade over my head, so I let her. I drink so much water. Then, even though I can barely stand, Dad hands me a bottle of André "champagne" and helps me up onto the bed of the truck. I turn around and look down at our group.

"What do I do with it?" I ask.

"Shake it!" he says. They've all got waxy blue cups courtesy of Tua, hopefully full of something better than this.

"To Miho!" Dad says. And they all cheer.

I shake the bottle and it sprays everywhere.

"Can I get down now?" I ask.

"You *may*, but *can* you?" X asks.

"I'm . . . not sure."

X helps me down. It's amazing that I can still walk. I feel so awake. All those miles haven't caught up to me yet.

And then my knees buckle. Wyatt grabs me before I hit the ground, and Rei pulls me back to my feet.

"You need to sit down," X tells me.

"I need to eat all the foods," I say. "And take all the showers."

I'm in dry clothes at last: lavender joggers and a brand-new *Almond Blossom* hoodie. Perfect post-race power costume. Rei had to help me change; I couldn't get my sports bra over my head. Having your best girlfriend help you put on underwear in the not-remotely-private cab of a pickup is a new bond that can't be broken.

As my friends break into my dad's barbecue and what they assure the grown-ups is their very first beer ever, I check my phone. My lock screen is overflowing with notifications, messages from friends I didn't know I had. The women from the tri club. The boys at the pizza shop. Kids I hardly know from school. A cousin in California texted to say they were following the live-tweet of my race.

What live-tweet?

I search online. It's easy to find: the first annual Miho-man. Updates, pictures, video. A ridiculous number of likes and retweets. I got a mention from the woman who won the world championship last year. All these people were cheering for me, and I didn't even know.

"Are you mad about the Twitter?" X asks, peering over my shoulder.

I take a piece of Hawaiian roll off his plate. I chew the tiniest piece. I put it back. Not happening. So nauseous.

"I'm not mad," I tell him. "It seems like it's about someone else."

"But it's not. You did all those things. And, one more thing . . . don't freak out, okay? This one is totally private," X says, handing me his phone.

"What is it?"

"We made an Instagram account when we first started and shared the username so we could show each other pictures. It's yours now. You can delete it or whatever, but you can also keep it and use it. If you want."

I scroll through the account they made. It's locked, and my only followers are my friends. It's moments I don't even remember, all those training day memories, snapped when I wasn't looking, my head down and sweat dripping off my nose. It's my graduation, my birthday hike, my dog being genuine internet gold. It's me wearing my very own Pipeline Tri Club hoodie in this giant shaka-throwing group melee around my bike. It's today. My friends with signs, the pig in the pit, Dad toppling the grill, my uncles. My family. Kyle, who changed the chalkboard sign at the shop to CONGRATULATIONS MIHO ON HER FIRST MIHO-MAN. It's me in the water, on the bike, running.

My finish line. The last picture is me and X, his arm wrapped around me, my shoulders draped with yellow tape, the perfect Hawai'i of postcards beyond us.

"It's all phony, like you always say. But it's also all real. So it's all as real as anyone else's phony," he says. "We thought you'd like to remember."

"Thank you," I say, giving his phone back.

"Does it feel real?" he asks.

"Yeah," I say, laughing. I gesture to my legs. "It feels real bad!"

"And Scumbucket?"

"What about him?"

"Did winning fix your broken heart?"

I smile. "I don't really believe in fixing anymore. I believe in change."

For a second I wonder what Scumbucket is doing. It doesn't hurt. It's something I can touch, pick up, and put down without falling down that hill of despair. The baby must be due soon. I wonder who he became this summer. I wonder if he's happy. He'll always be out there, but it doesn't matter to me anymore.

The wind picks up and starts blowing tents away. We rush to help secure hot dog buns and loose beer cans.

"The time has come to reveal the bets," Wyatt says. He hands Rei a sealed envelope, which she looks through. She smiles and clears her throat.

"Bets were closed this morning before the race began. Shall we begin?"

"Yes!" we all shout.

"Mr. Oshiro. Fifteen hours. Mr. Bu. Fifteen hours. Mr. Kalani. Fifteen hours."

"Hey!" my neighbors shout.

"Uncle Tua. Ten hours. Optimistic, Tua!"

"I'm putting 'Pizzas delivered by the winner of the first annual Miho-man' on the door," he tells me.

"Please no," I say.

"Oh yes. We can put 'Official pizza of Miho-man' on the signs too."

"Ahem," Rei says before I can protest. "Mr. Miho's Dad. Eleven and a half hours."

"Close!" I say. "That's gotta be the winner."

"Well, let's see. Lani. Fourteen hours. X. Twelve hours. Rei. Thirteen and a half hours. Kyle. Thirteen hours. Oh, shoot, can someone text Kyle? He asked me to send him the finishing time."

"What about me?" Trinity asks impatiently.

"You bet nine hours, you psycho."

"Obviously, I believed in you the most," Trin tells me. I want to hug her, but the thought of standing brings tears to my eyes.

Rei continues. "And Wyatt. Sweet Wyatt. What was your bet?"

Wyatt unfolds his piece of paper with a smug grin and shows it to me.

"Are you serious?" I hold it up so everyone can see.

"Eleven hours and eleven minutes," Wyatt says. Everyone applauds.

"He was off by three minutes," I say. "That's bananapants. How is that even possible?"

Wyatt shrugs. "Statistics, bitch."

~

My friends head home as they start falling asleep, first Wyatt and Rei, then Lani and Trinity. I watch as Lani and Trin walk toward Lani's scooter. Lani slides her hand into Trin's back pocket, and Trin puts her arm around her waist, and it's . . . perfect. Exactly the way Lani wanted it: no big deal. X stays until the bitter end, when my dad sends him home with a stern warning to stay awake at the wheel. I try to help clean up, but I can barely walk, and my brain is loopy. All I can do is eat. Now I'm starving. Tua keeps dishing up plate after plate while everyone cleans.

Soon it's just me, Dad, and Achilles on the beach. Achilles puts his nose under my hand, and something in his mouth squeaks. I take his toy from him. It's a pink rubber pig that makes the world's worst noise when you touch it.

"What's this?" I ask. I toss it away with what's left of my upper body strength, and it squeaks every time it hits the ground, then screams as Aki snaps it out of the air.

"Aki's new favorite toy," Dad says. "I gave it to him this morning to keep him away from the barbecue. Hasn't put it down yet."

Aki brings it to Dad, who throws it. I can hear Aki joyfully chewing it all the way down the beach, each chomp making it squeal.

"Ready, my flower?" Dad asks.

"Coming," I say, holding my bike and looking out over the ocean.

"Bring your bike," Dad says. I want it to be the last thing to go into the truck.

I am standing absolutely still, my bike in my hands, and the world is there. I can't see it, but I know it. It feels like anything is possible.

I'm sad my race is over. But a race is more than a day. It didn't start today. It won't end with this perfect night.

I grip my handlebars and stare out into the night. The wind sings in my ears and shows me the way forward.

I'm still racing. I always will be.

Acknowledgments

This book truly required a #supportcrew. I would like to thank:

My agent, Lucy Carson.

My editors, Wendy Lamb and Dana Carey, and everyone else at Random House Children's Books for their wonderful work on my novel.

My family, for their support.

My friends at American University Library, for their patience.

I would particularly like to thank Mom, Jeff, Dad, Sally, and Ethan for their service as race Sherpas.

Rikesh, Ruth, Ethan, and Mom for reading drafts and providing feedback. Dudley for carrying the wake-up-call banner.

Finally, a special thank-you to Ironman volunteers the world over. I'd give each of you a red wristband if I could. And to my fellow triathletes, who inspire me every day.

ABOUT THE AUTHOR

TARA WILSON REDD, a graduate of Reed College, grew up all over the United States, including in St. Louis, Seattle, and Central Oregon. A lifelong runner, she finally caught the triathlon bug and completed her first Ironman in 2019. She lives in Washington, DC, where she works in libraries (when she's not on her bike). *The Museum of Us* was her first novel.

TARAWILSONREDD.COM